# Wishless

*To Claudia—*
*Thanks for*
*reading*
*Louise Caiola*

## Louise Caiola

L & L Dreamspell
London, Texas

Cover and Interior Design by L & L Dreamspell

This is a work of fiction, and is produced from the author's imagination. People, places and things mentioned in this novel are used in a fictional manner.

ISBN:      978-1-60318-320-8

Library of Congress Control Number: 2011931750

Visit us on the web at www.lldreamspell.com

Published by L & L Dreamspell
Printed in the United States of America

# Acknowledgements

I am ever grateful to Lisa and Linda for giving this little story its wings to fly. Thanks to Cindy Davis, the fiction doctor—"take two mudslides and call me in the morning"—for her patience and keen editorial eye.

Thank you: to my agent, Terrie Wolf for inviting me to join her team of amazing authors.

To my parents, Nick and Fran without whose love and incredible generosity I would be up a giant creek with no paddle.

To my incredible kids, Melissa and Nicholas. You guys make my job worth doing well. We'll be Miley fans forever, won't we?

To Eddie, You always said it would happen. Thanks for believing in me endlessly with that great big heart of yours.

To Mary Kiernan Tighe, my dearest friend and kindred spirit. This journey was as much yours as it was mine. There aren't enough thank yous in this world...

To the extremely talented writer and author Patricia Crisafulli. Thanks for being the first person to give my writing a platform "out there." It is a great pleasure calling you my friend.

Shoutouts to the supporting cast: Chris, Steve, Stephanie, Marissa, Joe, and Steph, and to Scott for all the free therapy.

Finally I thank God for among other things, the gift of the written word.

To my grandmother…for that time she liked my really bad haircut. I miss you, Gram.

## The Big S

With the edge of my thumb wedged between my teeth, hot mustard on my tongue, breath trapped behind my tonsils, I was thinking, Jiminy Cricket, one year, speed. My grandmother, with the interstate mapped on her palms, took hold of two fortune cookies. I chose the one on the left. She gave me the other. I told myself it was just a stupid greasy biscuit, and not a crystal ball. I cracked it in two and peeled back the tiny curl of paper. It said, "You will live a long and happy life."

Those damn things were never right.

It's no problem. We all have a number, our calling card to the great beyond, which coincides with our allotted days on this great planet earth. If Doc Abner knew anything about anything then mine was 6752, give or take a few. I got sick when I was a little over 16. Most of the girls I knew at that age got one-up parties, where outdoing each other was a must, and in-your-face gifts like diamond stud earrings and in the case of one girl from school, a cherry red Mustang convertible.

Me? I got sarcoidosis. Long, boring disease. Considerably painless. Considerably terminal. Not in most cases. However, I am not most cases. I am the Exception.

I still remember how I felt the day I got the news. No longer human, in that moment I was a steel gray cloud, suspended in mid-air, wringing tears like so many angry, terrified raindrops. And then, after that I felt relief.

I would be with my mom again. It's what I'd been wanting for so long.

*"When your heart is in your dream, no request is too extreme."* From Pinocchio—the classic hook, line and sinker of hope.

☆

Doc Abner was nervous because I smiled. He was so cute. Like 60, five-foot-five, five-six if you account for the world's worst toupee on top of his head. He thought I was loony, still does. Every time we meet I make him tell me again, for the sport of it. On our last visit, one month ago:

"What do you think, Doc?"

"It's hard to say how long you have, Francesca. I'd be God or I'd be guessing if I did."

Doc Abner's hair was crooked as usual. As he leaned over me with his moth ball jacket and stethoscope bathed in rubbing alcohol, I thought his wig would topple forward and land right on my chest.

"Be God," I said.

"Excuse me?" He straightened up, adjusted his tie and lifted a hand toward his scalp. He had a thin line of lint in his neck fold and two chins. Both of them jiggled.

"Guessing is fine."

His face turned light crimson; his voice went unsteady. "Twelve months, maybe more, maybe less. You're the *exception*, got yourself a diabolical strain. I'm so sorry."

I faked an unaffected shrug and a grin. "Everyone has to die."

Seriously, I wasn't out of my mind. It sucked. Mostly 'cause there were so many things I hadn't done yet and wouldn't ever, if Doc Abner knew anything about anything.

But there was no sense in wasting precious time being bitter, not when there was a plan in place. It wasn't my idea. My mother came to wake me at 2 a.m., shortly after I found out about the Big S, in her dreamy way, all silver screen lit, far off and close at hand. It's how we communicated ever since she died six years ago. No matter what you might think, it's *true*.

She looked exactly the same: long, shiny waves in her walnut colored hair, her left eye pinched at the corner. An easy smile.

"Chessie"—it's what she used to call me, what most everyone calls me—"collect your wishes. Choose them carefully. Make a list, start with three or four. If you want them badly enough, they just might come true."

"My wishes? I don't know what they are." I stretched my hand out for hers, but there was nothing to touch, only a warm spot of gardenia scented atmosphere.

"They're inside you, Chessie. Don't be afraid. Opening your heart doesn't mean it will break."

"How? I don't know how."

She didn't answer. She would always make me have to figure stuff out all on my own. Nothing had changed since she'd been gone.

"Trust yourself. You're stronger and smarter than you think."

"I miss you so much, Mama. I'm scared."

"Don't be afraid, my darling. You'll be fine. Don't be afraid."

With her words I gave fear a shove and set off in search of my deepest desires. I also made a vow that nobody, other than my grandmother, would ever know I was sick. It would make things weirder than they already were. Everyone would greet me with that dreary, helpless, *Oh, that poor, poor girl face.* And even if they never said so out loud, I'd know exactly what they were thinking.

Chessie Madrid is the girl who can't escape death.

Not so. I'm the girl with four wishes, offered from the lips of my very own angel.

The morning that followed the visit from my mom I tore a sheet out of a half-used spiral notebook and began.

*1) I wish for a brother or sister.* Okay, really a sister would be cooler. Someone to tell me I'm wearing too much mascara, or too little. She might be handy for doing the things sisters do, like sharing sweaters and secrets. "I won't tell Gram you smoke, if you don't tell her I snuck out last night." But for seventeen years, two weeks and three days I've had to go it alone. Using too much or too little mascara, wearing my own sweaters and keeping my own secrets.

This was an old wish. A ridiculous wish. Surely you couldn't conjure up a sibling from mere longing any more than you could change the color of your eyes. Yet, there it was in first position.

*2) I wish a boy would fall in love with me.* Well, not any old boy. My best friend Meg's big brother, Johnny. Twenty, just finished two years of college, and recently moved back home. I hated his girlfriend for the simple fact that I wasn't her. Meg had no idea I was crazy about Johnny. If I told her she'd roll her sharp blue eyes and cough up a laugh. She said he's built for speed, not comfort. But, speed, in my case wasn't necessarily a negative. Meg also had no idea I kissed him once during a New Year's Eve party—my first—when someone suggested playing Seven Minutes in Heaven. She wasn't in the room when he and I crept quietly into the nearest closet, his long lean legs leading the way, his lips waiting for mine. His mouth tasted like beer and original flavored ChapStick, which became my new favorite romantic combo.

This was not merely an erotic wish. It was emotional too—I swear it. Johnny was the absolute hottest guy in all of Eden's Pond, Missouri. Second place on the list. Securely.

*3) I wish I could make my father suffer for his sins.* Mark Madrid, AKA Alan Lowenstein, Jr., the man who was technically my dad but only as a technicality and not one iota in the true sense of the word. M.I.A. for most of my life. A fake, a phony, and a fraud. He didn't even like himself enough to commit to being the person he was born, a Jewish boy, the son of Hedda and Alan Lowenstein, Sr. A trip to Spain when he was the exact age I am now gave Mark the inspiration to reinvent his persona. The only authentic thing about him was that he was genuinely a rotten ass.

This was a solid choice for third spot on the list. That was as far as I got on that morning. I kept thinking of lame, obvious wishes—trips to Europe, buckets of money for GG to live on once I was gone. Yet they weren't special enough, so I didn't write them down. I decided to sleep on it, maybe talk it over with my mom the next time we spoke.

Trouble was she hadn't come back. The wish list went quiet. I folded the page and stuck it inside the spiral notebook, which ended up buried beneath my gym shorts in the corner of my room. I carried on with the business of being pretend-well. That meant going to my job at the Dairy Maid as if it mattered at all, which it certainly did not. Like last night when I worked until closing.

I'd finished my shift, flew home, shrugged off my uniform, balled it up and tossed it onto the floor when my grandmother, GG, arrived at my bedroom door.

"Francesca," she began with a warning about my poor laundry habits, which she didn't have to elaborate on. Just the tone in her voice when she spoke my name, my birth I-mean-business name, was enough.

"I'll pick it up," I said.

"That's fine. I have news." She ran a shaky hand over the edge of my bed, straightening out the puckered squares in the pink cotton quilting then bending at the waist to sit carefully on the mattress.

GG wasn't really one for drama so I was careful to notice the stagy punctuation in her words. It made me sit too, on the vanity stool in front of my mirror, my rear end landing on a small stack of clean T-shirts that I had yet to file in my dresser drawers. "What? What news?"

She took a sigh, fidgeting with the tissue she had secured beneath her watchband—*Never know when you'll need to blow*—and drew her eyes down. GG wears her glasses almost all the time now even though she's only 65. She insists age has nothing to do with it, that she's been blind for as long as she can remember. They make her lashes look like two giant caterpillars having a snooze.

"GG…" I prompted with a knock of my foot.

"Chessie, your father is a hugely complicated person."

"This is news?" It is not.

"Infidelity was among his many inadequacies."

"Are you saying he cheated on my mother?"

"I am, and he did. Probably more than once, and yet your mother carried right on loving him."

"So he had affairs, and Mom knew about it. I already know that too." I grabbed a pair of sweatpants from the floor and folded them in half.

"Yes, well, one of those affairs resulted in a child."

I felt my heart go beat, beat, skip, beat. I squared my gaze with GG's, staring directly past the caterpillars and into her dark green eyes. "Mark has another child?"

"He does. Her name is Logan and she's seventeen. Her mother passed away last year, and since then she's been living with her aunt. But the woman's had some trouble with the law recently, and she's going to prison for a while."

It struck me that GG may have possibly been making a joke at my expense, concocting an outrageous story to see if I'd buy it and then ending with a "Gosh, Chess, you are so gullible."

"GG, are you for real?" I scanned the carpet for my notebook. Perhaps she'd discovered it along with a new warped sense of humor.

"This is not my idea of humor, Francesca. This young person is in need of a decent meal and a warm bed. She's coming to stay with us for a while. She needs a home, and we have one don't we?"

GG made most things as basic as they could be. We did have a home and right then I discovered I had a sister who would be sharing it with us. My stomach went loopy like that time I rode the roller coaster at the Edenville County Fair right after I ate a chili dog. I turned to stare at my own reflection in the mirror. I never did outgrow those baby doll dimples carved like two commas into the sides of my cheeks. With my mother's eyes, light hazel, and close set, and my overgrown hair GG said resembled a wig people wear for Halloween when they dress up as Pocahontas. Would she look anything like me?

"Don't we?"

"Yes GG, we do. When will she be here?" I had so many questions but I figured they would keep.

"In about three weeks." GG rose to go, padding softly across my green shag carpeting in her old terry cloth slippers. She paused and turned back, one hand on the doorknob. "Oh, and Chessie?"

"Hmm?"

"She's black."

"What?"

"Logan. Her mother was black. You'll straighten up in here, won't you?"

I said I would but I didn't. As soon as GG went downstairs I spun around in giddy circles and tore for my measly wish list. There it was, numero uno. Maybe I was dreaming now. Or, maybe I had already died. Yet there hadn't been a white light, no stifling sensation, no gripping pain and no choir of angels. Most of all there hadn't been a sign from my mother that she was coming to collect me.

I was 100 percent, unequivocally alive. And all at once I was meeting the realization of my first wish. Suddenly and for just one minute it struck me that sometimes, maybe fortune cookies don't lie.

# Show Me

I ate a bowl of cold cereal the next morning even though GG made eggs, sunny side up. I was in a hurry to get to Meg's and fill her in. I knew she wouldn't believe me. If anyone was from Missouri, it was Meg Lauten. She'd say, "A sister, a *black* one? Show me."

I drove my haunted '91 Dodge Shadow to her parents' house, in spite of the fact that it was only around the corner from mine. It was Meg who first discovered the Shadow was still otherwise occupied by its former owner, Mr. Henry Delafield, who died after having driven it to and from church services for two years. GG played bridge with the widow who sold it to us after her husband had his fateful massive heart attack. Mrs. D complained that her husband loved that "rotten bag of metal bones" more than her. Meg said you could smell his stale cigar in the upholstery so that must mean the old guy had refused to give up his wheels.

I was pretty sure it was just the odor trapped in the gray plaid fabric and not poor Mr. Delafield.

Meg's bedroom made mine look spotless. Her graduation dress, complete with sweat stains beneath the arms, was looped over the top of her closet door; the pantyhose she'd stepped out of one week prior were fermenting in place below. I'd be willing to bet that's where they'd stay till they began to resemble a science project gone wrong. It turned out she believed my story mostly because she knew GG wouldn't lie.

"This is actually pretty cool," she said while she arranged

her collection of lipsticks along the top of her nightstand, reds to fuchsias to peaches.

I hitched my shoulders, taking a tube of pale pink called Blushing Bride and running it slowly over my mouth. "I guess so, but it's bizarre, the fact that I've always dreamed of having a sister and now I do."

Meg twirled her ashy red hair between her fingers. "Johnny's girlfriend's half brother is a Puerto Rican."

"So?"

"I don't know…we don't have many around here."

"Many what?"

"Puerto Rican people, or blacks for that matter. Well there is that one family on Seventh Street." Meg was twirling her entire body then. She took ballet for ten years until she grew to be nearly six feet tall and far less graceful than she hoped to be.

"She's really only half black."

Meg stopped and cocked her head to one side.

"So, does that count?"

"For what?" I asked.

"If Logan has to fill out a census form, which box does she check—Caucasian, African American—which? She's neither."

"Actually she's both, Meg."

"Then I guess she counts twice," she concluded and went back to her twirling. Inside I was reeling too. In that instant in Meg Lauten's bedroom on a muggy Monday morning in June, I felt bigger than all the conversation and all the speculation and bigger than myself. My world was expanding from the inside out. For the first time in a long time, I didn't feel defined by some bully disease camped out in my lungs. I was somebody's sister.

"I'll bet she steals the attention of everyone, especially the boys," Meg decided with a final twist and leap.

Just like that I was small again, still eighteen, still unsure how my life would unfold. Would there be enough time to get to know this girl whose dad matched mine? Something in my brain fed me tiny morsels of hope. Maybe Doc Abner was wrong and

I wasn't the Exception. Maybe the x-rays were wrong. Maybe it was all a colossal mistake, a mis-diagnosis or a near-miss that meant I would live a little longer, like 60 years longer. I wanted to believe that, but I'm from Missouri too, and there just wasn't enough solid proof.

Meg and I headed into Edenville to go shopping for bathing suits. We didn't talk much more about the sister that may or may not be, except for when Meg declared that Logan was probably fat.

✵

Nothing much happens in Edenville. Less than that happens in Eden's Pond, the tiny annex of the village where I've lived forever. About five years ago we had an infestation of cicadas. It was so bad you couldn't sleep with your windows open or the noise would keep you up all night. People were talking about it so much that it made the local paper. "Eden's Pond plagued by hundreds of Uninvited Visitors!" the headlines screamed. Then there was the time the Kwik Stop was robbed. The folks here were pretty freaked out and suddenly front doors were locked where once they weren't. It turned out the police caught the boy who did it. It also turned out that Mrs. Delafield's nephew had a little too much time on his hands and a new drug habit to support. This piece of gossip made the cicada story seem downright silly.

For the most part, excitement in Eden's Pond was hard to come by. So twenty years ago when a strange man appeared out of nowhere with a long pony tail, reeking of hashish and English Leather, and rocking bell bottom jeans, the excitement was palpable. GG said you could hear the whispers for miles around. It's one of the stories she didn't like telling, though she did it anyway, if I asked enough to annoy her.

"Don't you dare do anything to embarrass me, Philomena," was how it began. It was the warning heard 'round the world, by everyone except my mother, Phillie Barraco Madrid.

"She had a mind of her own—nobody could tell her what to do—until HE came along. I knew right away he was no good, but your mother, well, he had a spell over her. She was only a little older than you are now Chessie, a bit more than a baby herself." GG would pause, reach out, and tuck her hand beneath my chin. Then she would twist her hankie and go on.

"I went up to her bedroom one morning and she had her suitcase out on the floor. Told me she was leaving with him. She was in love. Thought I didn't know what that was like. We had a terrible fight, something we almost never did. Not until then. Not until him. Later that day, he came knocking on the door asking me to reconsider my position. He was thick with charm, but I wasn't buying it. No sir."

GG would wave a pointed finger through the air, back and forth, to help make her point, shifting in her seat like her pantyhose were bunching.

"The next morning they were both gone. Just like that. Gone. He stole my only child. He was no better than a common criminal to me, a kidnapper. After seven days of quiet hell, without a word, she calls to say she married him. Can you say nightmare, Chessie?"

Could I say it? I'd say so.

✴

Meg was drifting in and out of the aisles of disarray in Sears. Bottoms and tops all mismatched. Two best friends also mismatched. She called commentary to me over her right shoulder. This one's cute, that one's God-awful. She was a long and lean Cheshire cat, stalking, hinting mischief in her stride. I stayed with her, faking attention and thinking how my mother ran off to Spain and got pregnant and married, or married and pregnant, the order not all that important anymore. It was my grandma's fear then that impressed me most. Fear that she'd never know me. Fear I'd be a little Spanish baby who'd call her once a month to say *hola*.

But Mom came back. We both did.

✴

GG liked this part the best, issuing a dry-lipped smile as she'd finish her tale. "Eight months later I stepped out onto the porch to get the morning paper and I found your mother sitting there with a big, swollen belly and bigger red eyes. It was the first time she discovered Mark had another woman, and she was devastated. Three days later and four weeks early, you came along. She went into labor while we were having our Sunday lunch. It was like you couldn't wait to get here, Chessie. You arrived before suppertime."

"In time for the pot roast," I'd add, because I knew she was going to.

"Yes, indeed! But you were born *here*, where you belonged and where you should have stayed. Yet he returned after six months passed, claiming to want to be a father all of a sudden and pretending he was done with her, with the other one. Your poor mother wanted to trust him and she did so in spite of herself. That's when you left, all of you, and went back to Spain. And I didn't see you again for three years, almost to the day, when she couldn't take it anymore. When his tales grew too tall for her to see past any longer. That's when I got my girls home for good."

★

I was only a toddler, barely old enough to form an opinion of my own, my memory hardly ignited. Yet now it was like a scrapbook in my mind, yellow-edged photos, colorless and out of sequence. At three-and-a-half, Mom telling me we were on a special adventure as we boarded the plane for the states. Mom belting me in beside her, in the seat nearest to the window, telling me we could count the clouds along the way. The feeling of gliding on wind, the power in the dips and pitches. And when we got caught up in a snag or bump, she'd called it the "airplane dance" so I wouldn't be frightened. The pilot emerging from the cockpit, long enough for a wave at the crowd of international travelers, as if he were a superstar. I was so young, so unaware, oblivious to the fact that Phillie Madrid kept her tears hidden behind a pair of dark sunglasses. I was entertained, enthused, then sleepy and at peace. She was heartsick yet hopeful that going home to Eden's Pond would make her forget all about Mark Madrid. Forever.

But it wasn't forever. It wasn't even for long. My mother tried to stop loving him. She just didn't know how. Forgiveness came easier to her than hatred. I remember the way she was willing to let bygones be bygones, evident by how she was ready to rush back to him a decade after their divorce when he said he still loved her and wanted to try again.

"He wants us, Chessie. We should give him another chance," she'd told me. It was like an eternity ago and yet like yesterday. She sat on the floor in front of me, her legs in a knot, her hair wet at the ends from her evening shower. She was practicing her yoga positions. She said it kept her centered. To me she looked wobbly. Even her words were wobbly. "What do you say? He's your father…"

"Oh really? Then where has he been all this time?" It troubled me now thinking of how easy it was for me to scold her for his actions. All she ever wanted was for us to be a family. Yet we weren't, and it surely wasn't *my* fault.

"People make mistakes, Chess. Not everyone gets it right the first time."

"Or the second or the third," I had said. I was twelve and a half, complete with all the acne and attitude.

"Just say you'll sleep on it." She made her request gently before returning to her half-lotus pose. I didn't say it, and I didn't sleep on it. Mark Madrid had hurt my mother. He pretty much said she wasn't good enough when he slept with somebody else. That translated loosely to "*You* aren't good enough, Chessie."

My mother took off without me, one week after he asked to, in her words, "Have a go at this reconciliation stuff. Don't miss me too much. I'll be home before you know it." It was raining the day she left. The cab driver brought an umbrella to the door. She rushed off smiling back over her shoulder as she bent into the car. I could plainly see the excitement in her eyes. It made me mad and sad all at once so that I didn't kiss her. I gave her a spaghetti arms hug and presented the side of my mouth. "I love you!" she bellowed from the window, down a fraction of an inch for the weather. I said it too. I know I did. Though she couldn't have heard since she was halfway to the airport by the time I replied.

☆

"Chess? Yo, Chess? Are you with me? You're like zoning out. Get the pink two-piece. Guys love that." Meg was modeling a tissue tied around her with dental floss and calling it a string bikini. Her boobs were the perfect size. Her waist was the perfect size too. And the miles of legs didn't hurt much either. But me? My body wasn't made for modeling anything.

"I don't know."

Meg shoved a hanger into my ribs with a teeny swimsuit dangling from one end.

"Try it on. Come on, you've got a great shape. Besides you only live once."

"True."

Inside the fitting room I stripped down and stared into the mirror. There wasn't one mark on my skin, one bruise or blemish. I looked completely healthy. It was all a giant misunderstanding. It had to be.

"Chess!"

"Okay, okay." I bought the pink bikini to shut her up. If I remembered correctly pink was Johnny's favorite color. And most of all, Meg was right. You only lived once.

# Bigger than Cicadas

Dairy Maid Employee Rule #1: Crap rolls downhill.

It was a slow night at work. I spent most of the hours killing time watching the customers come and go, not really serving anyone. I kept leaving things to the newest trainee, some kid from Edenville named George; got away with it because the manager didn't come in. So I sort of pushed George around, but not in a mean way. I was just a little distracted by what the next twelve hours would bring. She was arriving by bus at noon. GG said we'd go to the station together to pick her up.

"How will we know her?" I asked this afternoon while we ate egg salad sandwiches together, GG's on rye, mine on white toast. The truth was I realized we'd probably know her immediately. There weren't too many black people who came here, particularly 17 year-old, half-black girls named Logan.

GG didn't bother to answer. I guess she realized it too.

A pimped-out ride screamed into the Dairy Maid parking lot, rock music pumping, kids spilling out the open windows. It jarred me back to the moment at hand. I knew the car right away and I wished my hair looked better. I wished I didn't smell like mayonnaise.

"Hey Johnny," I said, suddenly wanting to seem busy or important, or both.

Johnny Lauten came in wearing a pair of jeans and a white T-shirt. Nobody wore a white T-shirt like he did. He offered me a small grin that said "I'm adorable and I know it."

"What's up, Chessie?"

"Not much." The inside of my mouth tasted like tin. A drum line played percussion in my chest. I could hardly hear the grumbling ice cream machine.

"Meg says you're getting a visitor soon. Some sister from out of the blue. Weird, huh?"

I nodded, adjusting my blouse. "Yep. She's coming tomorrow, actually."

"Deep," he said. He said that a lot.

"I guess. Can I get you something?"

"A cheeseburger. I'll have a cheeseburger and fries, to go."

"Sure." I sprang into obedient server mode, willing to take charge once again and forgetting that I had been bossing George around a few minutes ago. George seemed confused too, though he didn't mention it. He watched from behind his black-framed glasses as I jumped through hoops to please Meg's big brother. Surely, if I gave him the best burger he'd ever tasted he would forget all about that scabby girlfriend of his and ask me out. I've imagined that one day, in my pretend-well world, I'd wind up being Meg's sister-in-law.

"How's Sara?" I asked as if I even cared. Fell off the face of the earth, did she? Too bad.

Johnny looked at me with eyes that were immediately suspect. "She's okay…"

I was aware of my body parts, each one feeling twice the size and too clunky to move. I wanted to be a gazelle or a swan or something far more graceful and confident. Yet I was a dopey girl in a dopey outfit at a dopey job making a dope of myself. A gawky silence hung in the air until, thankfully, a new crop of customers arrived and Johnny's food was wrapped and ready.

"Here you go."

As I took the bills from his hands, my fingers grazed his. It was over then. I was gone.

"See ya." He took the bag and moved away. I was transported back to the closet again, *our* closet, until George dropped a tray behind me snatching me from my trance. As soon as Johnny was outside I swung around to see what had gone wrong. George stood there trying his hardest to become one with the walls.

"What *is* your problem?" I asked.

"Nothing, it slipped. Sorry."

I sucked my teeth and let him have a fresh lungful of my impatience. "Clean it up, and hurry," I said, making an amazingly smooth transition to fearless leader.

"Sorry," he repeated, reminding me that maybe I was being a little mean to him after all. He scrunched to his knees and began picking up the mess. I joined him even though I didn't want to. That's when I heard him again. Johnny returned, and he was looking down at me as I sat on the dirty tile floor in a pile of onion rings and lettuce gone wild.

"I need ketchup," he announced.

"Oh, okay, sure." I got up and abandoned George, my duties, and my manners. I grabbed a handful of packets, possibly twenty or more, and held them out to him. Johnny smiled and choked down a snort.

"Can I get a bag for them?"

I complied. No words. Just Robot Girl at his command.

For a minute he stared as if I'd turned blue or something, a *'What's with this chick'* look that made me squirm. And then he probably felt bad 'cause he broke out one of his famous lousy one-liners. "Hey, did you hear about the two peanuts that went into a bar? One was a salted."

I dredged up a laugh to show him I appreciated the effort.

"Hey… good luck with your sister. Meg says she's black. That's bigger than cicadas."

"Yeah," I said as he walked off. "Thanks."

So the bar was set, right then by Johnny Lauten in the Dairy Maid at 8:45 p.m. In Eden's Pond, the saying goes, if it's something with the potential to be huge, then it's bigger than cicadas. It might even prove better gossip than when Mark Madrid kidnapped my mother and took her off to Spain. What would they say when Logan Madrid came riding into town in the back seat of my haunted Dodge? Chances are they'd be talking. GG would be sure to comment on how you could hear the whispers for miles around.

By the time I was done with Johnny, George had finished cleaning the floor. All that was left to do was let forty-five minutes pass until I could go home. I wondered what Logan was doing just then. Was she putting her clothes in a carryon bag and saying goodbye to her old life? Was she wishing that she weren't? Maybe she had a boyfriend, one without a girlfriend named Sara. And maybe she had no clue that her arrival was being hailed as the next big thing in a silly small town.

✴

GG hummed through her happiness. I awoke at 9:30 the next morning to the aroma of pecan pie and the sound of GG humming a tune. The message was clear.

I didn't hop out of bed. I lingered there staring out the window where a foggy stream of sunlight poured in. The very early hours of this day brought a thunderstorm with claps so loud they sent long, angry hands into my room to shake me from my sleep. It wasn't right that I should be afraid of them at my age. That was kid stuff. Yet the eerie strings of lightning followed by the raging booms made me seek refuge under the blankets where I'd buried my head waiting for it to blow over. I was surprised I'd slept at all considering the weather and the circumstances. But I did, and I had to conclude that perhaps my sleep was a place of refuge too.

Soon enough I joined my grandma, still in her housecoat, giant silver curlers secured with big silver clips to the sides of her head directly above her ears, looking every bit the mid-western alien. She smiled at me as I took a seat at the table, the one closest to the refrigerator.

"I have hotcakes," she said, revealing a stack surely meant to feed half the population of Eden's Pond. When GG was nervous she did things in massive quantities. I wasn't hungry, although I knew if I didn't eat she'd file that stack in the trash in its original form without one bite missing. Then GG would break into her usual speech, the one about starving children in some third world country. I ate a cake and a quarter on their behalf.

"How did they find us?" I asked, careful to swallow first.

GG tipped the forks into the drain with a boisterous clank. "Who dear?"

"Logan's family. How did they find out about us?"

She had her back to me, but I could see her shoulders pull together and tense up as she spoke. "Apparently your father's gone missing again. Logan's Aunt Vicky has been trying to contact him for about a month. She did some research and it led her to our door, Mark's last known address before Spain."

"He never lived here," I argued.

GG spun on her heel to face me. "He's a liar, Chessie. Simple as that."

Her lips were thin and straight, her brows scrunched up in the middle of her forehead just beneath her bangs, which were teased and sprayed and locked in place. She'd had a dye job a week before so her hair was Elvis Presley black. In an instant her lips got full again, her brows spread over her eyes and her tone changed. "It's all right, sweetheart. This young lady has nobody to take care of her. She's a victim too."

"Like me, you mean?"

GG pulled the chair out with her left foot and slipped down into her seat. Her entire frame went soft as she reached for my hand. "Of course not. You've had a real rough go of things but you're nobody's victim."

Aside from Doc Abner and me, GG was the only person in the world that knew about the Big S. When she found out she held me in a vice grip so tight my sides hurt for days after. She refused to accept that I might have to leave her.

GG continued, not skipping a beat. "I thought we should leave by eleven-thirty. We don't want to be late and have her standing there waiting all alone."

"I'll be ready." I rose to clear my place.

"Good girl," GG replied. Yes, I was.

✦

The air conditioner in the Shadow coughed an asthmatic breath in our faces. GG's old sedan gave up on her over the winter, and she hadn't gotten around to having it fixed yet. She liked to ride the bus or have me drive her to the places she frequented most, the beauty parlor, the bingo hall, the grocery store. It was nearly 90 sweltering degrees already and my pink cotton shorts were sticking to the back of my legs as I sat behind the steering wheel, eyes straight ahead. GG fanned herself with a college brochure Meg left on the floor next to a chewing gum wrapper and two stray dimes. I played with the radio, twisting the knob to find a good station, while my grandmother spewed on about Mrs. Delafield's upcoming knee operation and how she wondered about the heat in Louisiana where Logan was coming from.

"I never did get to visit down that way," GG mused.

I hated to remind her that she'd hardly ever ventured beyond the borders of Edenville, or even much past the front gate at 1636 Lilly Lane. By the time we arrived at the bus depot, the sun had taken a smoke break behind a row of thin clouds. GG checked her watch over and over until I nudged her that the bus had pulled into the terminal with the hiss of a gassy steam radiator. My eyes shifted back and forth between the unloading passengers and my grandmother, who mindlessly ran her fingers over the sides of her head. I personally didn't see a reason to fuss. Right before we left the house I threw my hair up in a ponytail while simultaneously slipping my feet into my white leather sandals with the mud stains near the toes.

"There she is, there she is." GG pinched my arm between her thumb and pointer finger. She pushed forward in the direction of the small crowd leaving me lagging behind as I searched the distance for the sight of Logan. I must confess the girl I found was not who I'd expected to see. I was struck by all the things Logan wasn't. She wasn't short or chubby or ugly or plain. Her hair wasn't kinky or wavy but shoulder length, straight and shiny blue-black. She looked as tall as Meg who had arrived in my head just then to complain about how my potential sister will steal all the boys' attention. I realized in my quick assessment, that Logan was nothing like me and I was stunted by how medium I felt, medium height, medium weight, medium looks. Medium me. And now there was Extreme Logan, setting a large suitcase down on the pavement, and managing a small smile.

In my notebook at home and in every silent wish I'd ever placed, I never bothered to discriminate. A sister was a sister was a sister. Yet right then, when we were about to come face to face, it seemed I should have paid more attention to detail. No matter.

It was a done deal. GG and I smiled back and stepped off toward her.

## The Un-Me

"Hello, Logan? I'm Ghita Barraco."

Logan took my grandmother's hand as I reached them.

"Hello," Logan replied. Her voice was low and throaty; her face as smooth and clear as golden maple syrup. There was nothing about her that said she had spent the entire night on a smelly old tin can bus.

"How was your trip? Oh, where is my mind? Logan, this is Francesca—but you can call her Chessie. And call me GG, please."

For the first time we made contact, physical contact, as I leaned in to say hello and she gave my shoulder a light tap. I had no idea what it was supposed to mean. Was it the way folks hugged in Louisiana?

"Hi Logan."

"How was your trip?" GG repeated.

"Fine. It was fine."

"Let's get the rest of your things," GG said.

"This is it," Logan revealed with a snap in her neck.

We fell silent then, a tongue-tied pause that lasted for what felt like an hour until we were at my car. She and GG then politely passed ownership of the front seat between one another like a hot potato.

"I'll sit in back," Logan said.

"No, take the front, I insist," said GG.

This went on until I thought I might scream. In the first place, GG never wanted to sit in back, never ever. So that was how it would be. Now that Logan was here things that were once standard operating procedure would be kicked out the window.

On our way home, GG filled the air with so much cordial conversation that I was certain she'd been up all night rehearsing, auditioning for the role of grandmother to the Queen. Logan replied with all the right answers, sounding much older and wiser than what she was.

"Chessie's just graduated from high school," GG announced.

"Oh? Yeah, me too," Logan said. I felt her look over in my direction, but I kept my gaze pinned on the road ahead.

"You did? I thought you were only seventeen." GG took the words right out of my arid mouth.

Logan nodded. "I am. I got put ahead one year when I was twelve."

You win, I said, from inside my head.

GG leaned forward. She had perky peppermint breath. "That's wonderful. You must be very smart."

"Yes, very." I added, not so much because I agreed but because I realized I'd only said two words, "Hi Logan," since I met her and for all intense and purposes she might have been thinking I was simple. The "Yes, very" was damage control.

Logan flipped her hand in the air. "Fifth grade was really easy, that's all."

It took another agonizing ten minutes until we arrived at our small three-bedroom bungalow. GG had one, I had another, and the third one was a sewing room. Now it was a sewing room/guest room/Logan's room. The telephone was ringing as we were on tour of the house, which had recently been freshly spit shined, waxed and scrubbed. I stepped into the kitchen to answer.

I heard Meg panting on the other end, whispering as if she could be heard over the wires. "What's happening? Did you get her? Did she show?"

"Yup."

"Well? Is it bad?"

I watched as Logan ducked her head to go up the stairs to

my room, her tall, lean structure climbing slowly. "It's worse," I proclaimed under my breath. "She's practically perfect."

Meg groaned. "I'll bet she's putting on an act."

"You can't *act* beautiful...can you?"

"Sure," Meg replied, "you can gob on the makeup and put tons of crap in your hair. It helps. What is she wearing?"

"Blue polo shirt, long denim shorts, white moccasins."

"Designer?"

"Don't know, don't think so."

I leaned up against the countertop. Logan didn't look like she was wearing any makeup at all. I wasn't sure about the hair, but it looked pretty clean and her clothes, just right, designer or not. Still, I wasn't about to burst Meg's bubble. Soon enough she'd meet Logan, and it would burst all on its own. After a minute or two I heard them coming down.

"I have to go. I'll call you tonight."

"Hey, don't forget the party at Shelly's later. Bring your sister. It'll be fun."

"I guess so. I don't know. Maybe. Bye." I hung up with my indecision. I barely knew this girl, and Meg wanted me to introduce her to the entire population of Eden's Pond under the age of twenty-five.

GG was chirping about lunch and breezing past me toward the table. I stole a look at my stepsister from Louisiana as she stepped around me and into the room. Her mother must have been gorgeous because Mark wasn't. Mark, her father—my father. I moved quickly to claim my seat, the one she was unknowingly heading for.

"You can sit here." I pulled out the chair to the left of mine, the one normally empty.

"Thanks, but I'd like to use the bathroom and wash up before we eat."

"Of course," GG said, reminding her of the way with a pointed finger until she was out of earshot. "Oh, she's a doll, Chessie. You two are going to become fast friends."

I'd been raised to trust her opinion, to trust her with my very life. If my grandmother thought Logan and I would be friends, then I should believe it. Yet, she'd been abstract for so long, she'd been an idea in my head, my own creation, until a short time ago. If I were being honest, the sister I envisioned up until then was nothing like this one. The fake one seemed more real than this living, breathing being suddenly here and claiming to be related.

"It's a little strange, that's all," I whispered. "And I'm just tired today."

GG ran a worried look past me and then chased it away when I shook my head. "I know this is a lot for you, Chessie. You've been a real trooper." She gripped the top of my hand and gave it a firm squeeze. "Do you need to lay down for a bit?"

I nodded. "Mind if I skip lunch?"

"You go ahead, dear. I'll sit with Logan until you're feeling better."

"GG, you won't—"

"I won't say a word. Don't worry."

Upstairs my head was buzzing, a low, heavy vibration. I fell into the pillow, wrapping the two ends around my ears to make it stop. Five minutes ached by as I rocked back and forth, back and forth. Thoughts churned in between the tremors. Why now? I'd almost never felt that way. What was happening? I got up, went to my dresser and opened the glitter and macaroni shells jewelry box I made in summer camp when I was ten. I fished out the tiny curl of paper, the one from the fortune cookie. I read it over and over. I tucked it between my fingers and brought it over to my bed. Eventually, sleep met me as I repeated the mantra to myself.

You will live a long and happy life.

✬

At 3 p.m. GG grabbed her quilted purse and headed over to Mrs. Delafield's for tea. Every day it was the same thing, tea at three except for on most major holidays. Once she took me along, and I sat outside in the garden with them as they sipped and clucked. That's when I noticed the pot plants in the corner of the yard—possibly leftovers from her nephew who was still in county lockup. I wondered whether the old lady tended to them and cut them back not at all aware of what they were, or if she knew but pretended not to know. Perhaps on most days at 3 p.m. GG and Mrs. Delafield were sipping tea and getting high.

We were alone then for the first time. Logan paced the short length of the hallway while I settled into the rocking chair in the front corner of the living room with the TV Guide. Melrose Place rerun, maybe General Hospital. In a matter of minutes she stopped in the doorway looking my way but not directly at me.

"She didn't know about you or your mother," she began.

I caught her eye, making her face me. "I'm sorry?"

Logan shifted her weight from one foot to the other. "My mother. She didn't know Mark was married when they first met. He never mentioned having a family. If he had she never would have…"

I shook my head. "You don't have to talk about this."

But she kept right on talking. She was waves pounding on the beach. I was sand.

"No. I want to. I want you to know she wasn't *that* kind of woman. As far as my mother knew, he had no wife or no child."

I set the magazine on the table next to me. "I'm sure your mother was a good person."

"She was a great person," she said, correcting me.

"What was her name?"

"Janet. Janet Matthews."

"So she never took his name? They were never married?"

Logan's shoulders dropped a little. "No."

"I thought your last name was the same as mine."

"It doesn't matter. He was never really a father to me anyway."

"Me either," I said, jumping on the discarded daughters bandwagon. And there it was again, that sentence-less, expressionless gap in time from earlier that I'd been dreading. I started to wish GG would hurry home from her pot party and rescue me. I tried to smile it away but stopped when I realized I looked ridiculous and a little scary. I tilted my head up, my eyes escaping out the window before I returned to her, but Logan had disappeared into the sewing room again. All at once, gone.

It occurred to me that this girl might become a replacement for me in GG's life. Ludicrous? Perhaps. Still, disturbing images filtered into my mind. Logan moving into my room. Logan taking GG to bingo or for groceries. The two making a rhubarb pie. Logan becoming the un-Chessie, the new and improved version of me, the one without a monster lurking inside of her.

Had I really wished her here? If so, what did that mean for the rest of my list?

I raced to my room, shut the door and opened my notebook. Wish #2 was there, staring up at me, just waiting for its chance at bat.

# Hate to the 100th Power

How could somebody hate a person they'd never even met? I wanted to be mad at Meg for making her decision based on practically nothing, but she based it on what I said and perhaps I was feeling a little guilty. Logan wasn't all that bad. Though when she declined the invite to the party saying she was too tired, Meg declared her a snot who thought she was above us. We sat on the back steps of Shelly's house that night where Meg downed her second beer. She made an excuse that it was still as hot as hell's best day and she had to keep drinking to cool off. I only reminded her once that Shelly had a pool so there were options.

"So she's sitting at home with your grandmother? Jeez!" Meg rolled her eyes up into her head until I saw just the white parts.

"Yeah."

"I'll bet before you know it, she winds up going back to Louisiana," she predicted while swirling the contents of her bottle until it made a Jacuzzi of yellow-brown suds.

"I don't think so. She has nowhere to stay. Her aunt is in jail now or something."

"Really? Think about it. If, God forbid, GG died or went to jail, where do you think you'd stay?"

I feared a trick question, and hesitated until she continued.

"*With me*, of course; with your best friend! Isn't it strange that this girl has no friends who were willing to take her in? Isn't it, Chess?" She laid her elbow on top of my knee.

"I guess," I shrugged. "I don't know. Maybe this was a last resort."

"Or maybe she's completely antisocial and has no friends."

Meg had out her bitch broom, making sweeping generalities. I felt oddly like a big sister who should be defending her sibling, though I didn't dare. I chose instead to change the subject, as I flipped her damp arm off me and then looked around the crowded yard, kids joined at the hip, others getting wet and wild.

"Are Johnny and Sara here?" I tried to sound nonchalant, blasé.

"I don't know. Who cares? He's such a jerk with her. All they do is fight."

"Really?"

"I don't know how she puts up with him. My brother is *such* a loser."

Says you, I was thinking. I'll take him. He won't fight with me; he won't be a jerk when he's *my* boyfriend.

"What do they fight about?"

Meg stood up. "I don't know. All sorts of stuff. The other day I caught something about sex. He wants to; she does, but she won't."

"She won't? You mean they haven't done it yet? No way!"

"Whatever. It's gross anyhow—the idea of my brother having sex with anyone is totally outer limits." With that Meg was off, rushing to mingle with Shelly and some others who had just finished taking a swim. I hadn't brought my suit along for two reasons: 1) I wasn't positive that I didn't look hideous in it and, 2) I had my period. I sat there on Shelly's back steps, alone and bleeding and lost in thoughts of Johnny and Sara and Logan, in that order, until the springs on the door behind me startled me from my daze.

"This party sucks," he said. It was *him*. Johnny took a load off right next to me. I fashioned a pit sniff out of a bored stretch. Deodorant and lilac body splash in check. I thought to move aside, but then thought again. I made some sound that was meant to agree with him and tried to recover.

"Are you here by yourself?"

He ran his hand through his hair, soft and sticky-bun blond. "Yeah. Sara and I broke up."

"Oh? Sorry."

"Nah, it's cool. It's all good."

I wondered if Meg would think it was doubly gross if her best friend had sex with her brother. It would be my first time. Meg had already done it twice. She said she doesn't understand what all the fuss is about.

"So did you have your new arrival yet?"

Something made me look down at my crotch, and Johnny smiled. "I mean, your sister."

"Oh yes, she's here…well, not here at the party, but here in Eden's Pond." I stared off at the next bunch of kids heading into the water.

"Aren't you going in?" he asked.

"No, no." I shrank back on the step.

"Why not?" I watched his eyes fall over the length of my body, thinking that I might spontaneously combust into the moment.

Before I could bluff my way through an answer, Meg shot me a look and then a shout. "Chessie, come here!"

Johnny ignored her. "Are you going to the Edenville playoff game tomorrow?"

"I'm not sure."

"You should go. They're in first place, could go all the way to the series. I'll be there. You should go."

I nodded while every inch of my insides jolted with excitement. I was a thousand helium-balloons floating on air. It was a done deal. A herd of hungry hippos couldn't hold me back. "Maybe I will," I said.

"Oh and hey, bring your sister. Meg says she's hot."

Just like that I lost my air. I was deflated, flat on my face. Maybe Meg was right about him being a loser after all. Maybe she was even right about Logan stealing all the boys' attention. The very idea of her had Johnny bothering to bother with me. I should have known. I got up from the stairs and trudged over to Meg, only because I was unable to dissolve into the atmosphere the way I wanted to.

✶

The following morning I managed to put on a happy face while I had breakfast with GG and Logan. It seemed they'd become "fast friends" while I was away.

"Did you sleep well?" GG asked—her, not me.

"Oh yes, thanks."

"It's wonderful that you like cranberry muffins. Help yourself to another. Oh, you too, Chessie." GG was wearing her royal blue checkered apron, the one she reserved for special occasions. I didn't know whether muffins with Logan constituted special, but I was guessing so. As they chattered on, I globbed two pats of butter on the edge of my plate for a bite and dunk. Logan carefully set a knife to her muffin to apply her butter in a thin, even layer. I ignored the prattle and quietly reminded myself what I *wouldn't* be doing in the afternoon. Then GG turned the conversation to me.

"Chessie, you should take Logan to the Edenville game today."

How's that?

"Is it a baseball game?" Logan asked, pouring a splash of grapefruit juice into her glass.

"Yeah," I said with an equal splash of pretend enthusiasm.

"Do you like baseball, Logan?" GG was hustling around the room so quickly I felt she might take flight. It was only ten a.m. and she was snapping the ends off a pile of snow peas.

"I was captain of my high school softball team," Logan replied. That would be a yes.

"*Oh*, that's wonderful! Isn't it wonderful, Chessie? Well, then you girls should head over to Edenville for the playoff. It'd be fun."

Logan looked my way with perfectly arched, raised eyebrows. "I'll go if you want to…"

"Okay, sure," I heard myself say, though for the life of me, I didn't know why. I glanced at the red clock on the wall, the one GG said was supposed to be an apple but it's a tomato if you ask me. I wondered if I could chew so slowly we'd miss the first few innings. When I turned my eyes up, I saw that for the first time since we met, Logan was smiling at me.

"Sounds good." She popped a third muffin into her mouth. If I ate like that I'd be five hundred pounds.

Yeah, it sounded real good, but only in backwards, upside down, opposite-of-good world.

✫

"So tell me, Logan…what do you all do for fun in Louisiana?" We had only been at Shaker Stadium for forty minutes and Meg was drilling Logan for thirty-eight of them. I had come to the conclusion that Logan must have studied boxing while she was in school since she'd been a formidable sparring partner for my very best, sweetest, most evil friend. As I sat there watching Edenville's star hitter steal bases, Johnny Lauten was stealing hound dog gazes at my little sister.

It was when Logan got up to get a soft drink that Meg lunged for my ear. "Well, I think she's a phony, a real wannabe. She *is* gorgeous, though. I hate to admit it. And, I think I can see a resemblance between you two, right around the mouth. No, the chin. You two have the same chin. I don't believe that bull about her best friend summering in Australia, I mean, who does that?"

The buttons running down her tight purple blouse gaped like fish mouths. She was wearing a purple bra.

"Anyhow, Chess, I don't think I'd trust her if I were you. In fact, I'd lock my bedroom door at night."

"Why? Do you think she's planning to rob my tons of jewels, my expensive wardrobe or the wads of cash I keep stashed under my mattress?"

Meg retreated and wrinkled her nose. "Why the sarcasm? I only want to help you, Chess. I have a vested interest. You *are* my main girl."

"Sorry, I don't know." I followed Johnny's eyes as he followed Logan while she walked to the stands. Random, painful thoughts shot through my head. They all said the same thing. He was going to fall in love with her, I knew it. They'd hold hands with braided knuckles and disappear behind the bleachers where they'd start something now they would have to finish later after it got dark. Oh God. Logan would have sex with him. Before I did.

I felt like I'd eaten boiled rats.

"So you gonna introduce me or what?" Johnny pushed his way over to Meg and me.

Meg unwrapped a piece of gum and shoved it into her mouth. "Get lost."

"Come on," he insisted, underscoring his urgency with an elbow to Meg's side. I was nothing but an invisible girl taking up invisible space on the bench. He hadn't even said hello. Logan stepped up to us, her long legs swallowing two rows at a time.

Meg did the honors with the excitement of the flu. "Logan, this is my brother, Johnny. Johnny, Logan."

"How are ya?" Johnny asked with a nod of his head.

"Nice to meet you," Logan said. She didn't seem immediately impressed. Perhaps she needed glasses. She moved past him until she was at the end of the bench next to me.

"Switch with me," he blew into the side of my head.

"What?"

Johnny motioned for us to trade places and because it was Johnny, I obeyed.

"I hear you're a pretty good ball player," he crooned to Logan in his let's-do-it voice.

"I used to be. I had to quit when I became the captain of the math team. We were called the Algebra Mathletes."

"Deep," Johnny said.

Meg took a hold of my hand and squeezed it—hard. When I swung my head to her she had her finger in her throat. "The Algebra Mathletes? Give me a break! I hate her to the hundredth power."

"Shh!" I warned.

A tie led the game into extra innings, twelve of them all together, and Edenville eventually lost 7-6. I lost too, and Logan had her win by default. I convinced myself Johnny was drawn to her because she was like Persia, vague, exotic and mysterious.

It wasn't until we were at home that I got up the nerve to ask her what she thought of him. She was peeling a banana skin and settling into a chair.

"He's okay…kind of obvious."

"Obvious?"

"Yeah, not my type really."

I spat a sigh of relief into the air from across the room where I was rinsing my hands in the sink. Meg and I had shared a lemon ice and the same gooey wooden spoon.

"Logan…how did she find out? How did your mother end up finding out about mine?" Maybe there was something in the water. I didn't know why I asked.

"She found the picture," she answered, matter-of-fact.

"What picture?"

"The one of you and your mother, the one he had hidden in his drawer. I still have it. Actually, I brought it with me. Thought you might want it." Logan got up and went into the sewing room, then came back with an envelope, which she handed to me.

I set it down at first to dry my fingers, and then released the flap. The photo was in black and white, vintage looking, older than it really was. There I sat, just a tiny thing leaning into my mother's lap. She was smiling big and wide, a lottery mom with her prize. Her arm was draped over my shoulder, keeping me close and safe. I forgot how bright she once was, how her eyes were shiny like drops of soft glass, and how her dark brown hair would crumple up, especially when it rained. I turned it over and there, in her fanciest cursive, it read simply, "Chess and Me."

"So she found this photo?"

Logan pulled her hair out of her face and nodded.

"I don't remember much about it. I was still really little. But I know she said he didn't deny you. He didn't make any excuses. He just said, 'That's my family.'"

I shook my head. "And yet we really never were…a family… not with him. It was my mom, me and GG."

"Your grandmother's really nice. You're lucky to have her."

"I know. What about yours?"

Logan and I moved to the table where we each took a seat.

"She didn't care for our father much. When mom took up with him my grandmother gave her an ultimatum. She demanded that she stop seeing him or else she'd never be welcome in her home again."

"Wow, that's funny. GG hated him too."

"Yeah…so when my mother picked him, basically, she was disowned."

I wanted to push for more, like what happened to her mother exactly and to her aunt in jail, but I couldn't stop hearing her say "our father" as if she'd been praying. I couldn't get past the notion that there we were, two strangers from the seminal pool of one man who had unknowingly created an unlikely sisterhood. And in the sunlight that came filtering through the kitchen window landing on her face, I thought I recognized a chin that did look a little like mine.

# Ragweed

GG was 35% deaf in her left ear. On account of that she couldn't whisper, even if she tried really hard, like she did that night at 8:45 p.m. in her bedroom, which was right below mine. She forgot about the heating vent on the wall next to her nightstand, and how it was like a megaphone. So I sat in the middle of the floor, picking at the twirled ends of my carpet and pretending not to hear. But I did.

"Is there anything new I should know, Doctor? Anything you didn't mention at our last visit? No, she seems okay…an episode here and there…nothing too alarming. What about that specialist in St. Louis? …Well, please, I'll do whatever it takes, go wherever we have to. You realize she's what's left of my world. Thank you, Doctor Abner. Goodnight."

I knew about her clandestine phone calls with him, the ones she didn't want me to know she made. With each one her voice grew more panicked, more desperate. To hear her say out loud that I was her world made me feel bad all at once for my little jealous rant about Logan. Surely Logan wasn't here to replace me, if it turned out the fortune cookie was wrong and I led a short and unhappy life. I thought of telling GG about Mom's visit and our plan and how she said I'd be fine. But come to think of it, just what did my mother mean by *fine*? Was she implying that I would beat the Big S at its own game? Or did she mean it wasn't such a bad thing to die and go live in heaven with her?

I used the leg of my desk to pull myself up. That's when I

heard her again. GG began another conversation. But this time, who? I sat again, slid my butt over to the wall and pressed my ear up against the metal grate.

"They're both here now…together…no, I don't know if I'm going to keep her, for God's sake, she isn't a lost animal, although then again she might as well be… I don't see why I should answer any of your questions. If you're so curious about them why don't you see for yourself? …Oh don't give me your boloney, Mark…"

My heart sent blood to my head and it whooshed loudly through my eardrums. GG was talking to him—to "our father" Mark Madrid, the he-man child hater. Only a few weeks ago she reported that he'd gone missing.

"…How do you know they won't see you? When was the last time you asked? Look, you have two lovely young ladies here who, for what it's worth, are orphaned. How typical of you to continue to turn your back on them!"

She was giving him hell and suddenly I was 35% deaf too, or she had moved away from the vent, which made a lot more sense. After a minute I heard her again.

"Listen Mark, there's only one reason I agreed to speak with you at all, and it isn't to catch up on old times… Yes, but that doesn't mean everything between us is water under the bridge… Okay I will, just as long as you understand that this is for the girls. Fine, goodbye."

I chased my pulse until I felt as if the room had stopped spinning. What reason did GG have to speak to him? She'd sworn him off years ago, even added his name to her list of least favorite persons. It went—in no particular order—Benito Mussolini, the devil, Mark Madrid.

I wanted to call Meg but she was at the movies with Shelly. She asked me to go. I faked a headache, mainly to avoid bringing or not bringing Logan. And what about Logan? Was she in her sewing-bedroom accidentally overhearing GG's loud whispers?

The only thing I could be certain of is that there was some plan in motion, and we weren't supposed to know about it. Not yet.

⭐

The next day I was scheduled to cover the lunch shift. The entire morning passed without a word from GG about her late night phone call. She did, however, mention quietly that I should see about getting Logan a part-time summer job with me. We were in the garden, just us two, her with the hours at her disposal, and me with twenty minutes to spare.

"I don't know. Why would she want to do that?" I was adjusting my nametag. It said, "Fran." Nobody had ever once in my entire life called me Fran.

"It'll give her some structure while she's here," GG said in her lowest loud voice.

"I don't know. She already seems pretty structured to me. So, I guess I'm gonna take off now. If anyone calls for me, anyone at all, you'll take a message right?"

"Of course, dear. But I'll be running out myself in a bit. I'm going to pick up some paint for the porch. It's chipping so badly. I ran into Mrs. Lauten yesterday, and she said her Johnny is looking to earn a little cash so I'm going to pay him to paint for us."

"What?" I heard her but still…what?

"I've hired Johnny Lauten to paint the porch. You know, Meg's brother. He's home from college now." GG looked up at me from her padded kneeler. She had a spade in one hand and a big smear of rusty soil across her forehead. She wore random wires of gray like tinsel on her head.

"Why him? Why don't you hire a real painter guy?"

GG furrowed her brow. "Chessie! What's wrong? Don't you like Johnny?"

"Sure, he's all right, I guess. I really have to go, or I'll be late." I stepped over her tray of yellow and orange marigolds, their bittersweet scent tickling my nose, and began to walk down the driveway before I turned back. "So you'll tell me if *anyone* calls or if anyone has called…"

GG waved her glove at me and quickly returned to her deeds. Now he'd be at my house every day, Johnny, Logan and me. And then on days like this when I was stuck swirling ice cream cones and cleaning out the deep fryer, it would be Johnny and Logan. How romantic.

✰

I stared at George, well not really *at* him, more like *through* him as he pushed a broom across the floor under the tables near the bathrooms. He was what some might call a geek, but I wasn't too sure. To me, he was part nerd, part puppy dog, sort of cute in a nipping, yapping way. All I knew was that he wore his dark brown hair parted way over on the right side of his head so his overgrown bangs were nearly always in front of his eyes. His clothes didn't ever seem to fit right; they were too big or too small, too long or too short and then his socks showed out the bottom. If I squinted, I could see the potential. George was like a lump of clay that *could* become a decent vase in the right hands. He didn't say a lot, didn't seem to stand for much of anything. I thought a guy should stand for something. I tried to imagine what Johnny Lauten's cause was. I figured he had to have one. Mark Madrid had a cause. He stood for the fight against monogamy. Why have only one woman when you can have two? I watched the random leftover fries pile up in the corner beneath the dirty yellow bristles. What did Mark stand for now? Did he have a new cause—perhaps a try-and-reconnect-with-his-children cause? And what part would GG play? George noticed me and presented a weird smile, like one side of his mouth was not in agreement with the other. I decided that George stood for clean floors everywhere. He needed a ride home and asked me if I could give him one.

"I'm not a taxi cab, you know," I replied, as we filled the napkin dispensers.

"Okay, never mind," he said.

And then I felt like a huge bully. "Well, it's no big deal anyway; I guess it'll be all right."

"I don't want to put you out or anything." He had crooked glasses or crooked ears. I wasn't sure which.

"I said okay, didn't I?"

As soon as our relief team arrived, George and I walked slowly to my car. I realized he had these lanky, racehorse legs and he could probably run home just as easily. At first, neither of us said much, but after a few minutes he cleared his throat.

"Chessie?"

"Yeah?"

"There's this teen dance thing going on at my father's golf club and I was wondering if maybe you wanted to go with me…"

"I can't. I have plans."

He sat forward in his seat, eyes piercing the side of my face. "I haven't told you when it is yet."

"Oh…sorry."

"It's next Saturday night…"

I stopped at the red light and looked his way. "George, the thing is…well…"

"It's okay. I get it. You have a boyfriend right?"

"Yes, I do. And he wouldn't want me dancing with somebody else." I was going to go with the "I don't date guys at work" speech, but this seemed equally good.

George nodded and sat back, his shoulders falling two whole inches.

"I don't know the way, George," I said softly.

"Huh?"

"The way to your house. I don't know where you live."

"Oh. You go up to Rockvale and take the first left, follow that around to Cherrywood, and then a right. I'm number 13."

"Rockvale is the street near the high school?"

"Yeah."

The quiet got so loud I had to flip on the radio to drown it out. He was sniffling a little and, when I glanced his way, he responded quickly, "Allergies."

"I get them too, mostly just when I eat horseradish or sesame seeds."

It took three more traffic lights and a right on Cherrywood before he spoke.

"Ragweed."

"What?"

"I'm allergic to ragweed. This is it. This is my house." He pointed to a big home, nearly twice the size as mine with a lush green lawn and rows upon rows of pink and white flowers all standing at attention. I'll admit, I didn't see it coming. If I had to guess I would have pictured he lived in the mobile home park behind the funeral parlor.

"Thanks," he said, grabbing the handle and springing out the door.

"Sure," I called, but his racehorse legs had already taken him halfway to his front steps.

✯

Logan had on a bright blue sundress with straps that tied around her neck. It made her creamy brown skin glow. I didn't wear sundresses all that often. For some reason, suddenly I wished I had. We were standing outside with GG as she held a paint swatch up to the side of the porch. It was called "Moroccan Sunset," but it looked pretty beige to me.

"What do you think?" she asked neither of us in particular. It seemed she'd already decided, since a gallon of it was waiting on the deck.

"It's nice, Ghita," Logan answered. She doesn't say "GG," even though my grandmother has continually insisted.

"Yes, it's nice," I sounded like a parrot, a copycat—bland, unoriginal.

"It'll do, I suppose," GG said.

"When will he start the job?" I asked, and I must have appeared too interested because Logan looked at me with a big question mark on her face. I never asked my boss about getting her a position at the Dairy Maid. I wondered if Johnny would hire her as his assistant, a painter's helper in a bright blue sundress.

"Tomorrow morning, weather permitting." GG climbed the two porch steps while holding the railing tightly saying "uh-uh" as she went. Her legs didn't match her middle anymore. They were thin, and the skin was all spotty, but you could only see that when she didn't wear her support hose. She lugged a round, squishy pillow in the center of her; "too much pie, too little youth," she says.

"They say it's going to be beautiful out," Logan remarked. "Good painting weather."

The sun bit at my shoulders, and I silently wished for a sky full of rain clouds to come. It wasn't that I didn't want to see Johnny. It was that I didn't want him to see her.

GG kept her back turned as she filled a small glass with lemonade from a pitcher where the lemons swam blissfully around inside. It looked like she was moving in slow motion when she slipped her hand down into the pocket of her apron, pulling out a sheet of paper, folded in fours. She then turned around to us looking down to where we were standing, as if she were on stage and preparing to address her audience.

"Girls…I got this letter in the mail a few days ago. It's from your father. It was addressed to me, so at first I assumed it was the usual money he sends. But it isn't for me. It's really for the two of you…indirectly anyway."

From the corner of my eye I saw Logan pull up a long strand of hair and wind it between her teeth.

"Would you like me to read it to you? It's fine if you don't."

While I was still busy with deciding, Logan piped up. "I do. I want to hear it." Her voice sounded the way it did the time she spoke to me about her mother.

GG looked into my eyes. "What about you, Chessie?"

And even though I wanted to say no, "I want to hear it too," came out of my mouth.

GG settled into the green plastic chair that's supposed to look like one of those expensive wooden Adirondack types. She opened the page, adjusted her glasses and dabbed mindlessly at her chin.

In that light of day, I saw the layer of fear just beneath the pressed powder on her cheeks. She took a moment to collect her thoughts, pausing and waiting for what, I wasn't sure. I only knew that my heart was racing, my fingers tingling, my breath suddenly choppy inside of my lungs where the lesions were still growing according to the latest set of x-rays. *The Exception.* I had the sensation of having been submerged under water just long enough so that I might lose consciousness. Instantly I imagined what it might be like to never see her again. It was equal parts terrifying and painfully sad. I blinked back a lone tear that was determined to escape from behind my lid and slide down my face.

Ragweed.

## The Devil's Details

"Ghita, I am unsure as I set my pen to this page, what I should say, or if I should say anything at all. Perhaps there are no words that will suffice. Perhaps there are too many. I understand circumstances have arisen lately that caused some distress. For whatever its worth, I am sorry for the trouble. I wish I could be the go-to guy, the one to throw out a line. But you know as well as I, that isn't who I am. That said, I am caught between those two extremes every day. Between who I am and who I want to be. I am a free spirit who wants to be a captured soul. I want to be trapped by my choices, yet I am emancipated in spite of them. I want to be a father, but I'm just a kid myself."

GG paused to pull in her breath. I watched it fill her chest, and I listened as she released it slowly. She stole one look at us, her loyal subjects, before she continued. "Chessie and Logan deserve better than the likes of me. They deserve so much more than I can offer. However I haven't forgotten each tender detail about who they once were. And I often wonder if they have grown into different people now. Does Logan still love strawberry ice cream with chocolate sprinkles? Does Chessie still giggle when she's scared? Ghita, with your permission I would enjoy the opportunity to speak with both of these young ladies. I fully expect and accept it if any one of you decide against it. And I thank you for being there for them. I'll be in touch. Blessings…Mark Madrid."

"I'm going for a walk," Logan announced, without a hint of what she may have been thinking.

GG strained to get out of the chair quickly enough to stop her. "Alone? Logan, you'll lose your way."

"No, I'll be fine." She twirled on her flip-flopped feet, her hair draping over her shoulders like a shawl.

My eyes followed her down to the edge of the lawn, until I realized I wasn't all that interested in where she was heading.

"Chessie?" My grandmother had a look of panic on her face; her cheeks drained of their usual tint. She was GG with the Moroccan Sunset skin.

"She'll be okay," I told her.

"And what about you?"

I reached into the pit of my stomach to scrape up what I could of a smile. "I'm okay, too." My butt was burning; my pants were on fire. Before GG was able to put the letter back into her apron pocket, I climbed the steps and held out my hand where she placed the paper. She did say it was ours, Logan's and mine, indirectly. And so, indirectly I would own it, if only long enough until I could stop wanting to throw up.

☆

My mother never did make it to the airport that day. The rain picked up. The cab driver reported it was hard to see but a few feet in front of him. It was four hours since GG read me his letter, the one I had since re-read forty-six times. I think I read it plenty, because I knew it by heart. Instead, I set it on my dresser next to my half-used bottle of Love's Baby Soft Body Spray, and I took hold of the photo of me and her, the one Logan brought. Instead, I looked into her eyes and wondered what she was thinking the moment the taxi crashed head-on into a tree. Did she have time to pray, to be frightened, to realize at all she'd never know her middle age, or even her next day? I had only one thing to say to my "father," Mark Madrid, who signed off with blessings now. No Mark, I don't giggle when I'm scared anymore. Mostly, I just cry.

He wants to talk to us, to the two young ladies that deserve better than the likes of him. I thought about my list and my wish in third place. To make my father pay for his awful behavior.

Could this be my big chance to have it come true?

I brushed my hair. Meg said that if you did 100 strokes before you sleep you'd never get split ends. I refused to decide a thing, not even what I planned to wear to greet our new painter in the morning. I had one last look at my mother and me, from so long ago when life was far less complicated and felt the water push at the edges of my lashes.

✮

Mother Nature was at her most sadistic between the hours of midnight and eight a.m. It was in that blissfully naïve time span when a forehead that went to bed naked can become the not so proud owner of a bright red and glowing pimple. I awoke, sprang from my white cotton sheets with the teeny rose buds, and rushed to the window where I was greeted by a royal blue sky. From there, things went bad to worse when I met myself in the mirror and discovered my new affliction.

"Great," I groaned to nobody or God or Mother Nature. If life was fair, Logan would appear at the breakfast table with an equally offensive spot smack in the middle of her forehead. But sixteen minutes later, as I watched her glide into the kitchen in a LSU polo shirt and jean shorts, I was certain Logan's legs had grown an inch longer and her boobs an inch larger overnight. Life, as I already knew, didn't bother with fair.

"Johnny Lauten should be here any time now. I wonder if he's eaten." Even my grandmother looked nicer than normal minus her customary curlers and housecoat.

Logan's hair was piled up on top of her head in a casual bun. I'd spent fourteen minutes trying to make my bangs stay put over the bump.

There were platters of scrambled eggs and toast being carted over from the countertop and placed before me. "What is it, Chessie? Why aren't you taking anything?" GG asked.

"I don't know. I'm not all that hungry," I said.

"Me neither," Logan added, sipping juice from a small glass. "I think I'm going for a run."

GG was frowning and searching out the window at the same time.

"If that's okay," Logan said, placing her hand on GG's left shoulder.

"Of course, dear. Do be careful."

Be careful? Of what, shin splints? Had anyone noticed my forehead? I was the one who needed to be careful.

"I'll have something when I get back," Logan declared and reached down to secure the laces on her sneakers. She didn't even bend her knees, simply stretched all the way over as if she were made of rubber. The front door banged closed behind her and she was out of sight in an instant. GG turned to me.

"Honestly, if I was your age and could eat all I wanted to without gaining a pound…" She wanted to be angry that she'd done all that cooking for nothing but I knew she was angry because she's thicker in the waist now than she wants to be. "Oh, here he is." I was grateful for Johnny's arrival, as it made her forget her attitude in the blink of an eye as she motored out the door to meet him.

I glanced at the wall where we have a wooden mail holder with two horizontal slots—incoming and outgoing. We got it at a garage sale in Edenville along with a set of bookends with one broken end. I got up and took a hold of the envelope, the one Mark's letter came in. It was the P.O. Box I looked at. He collected them. This I could only surmise by the various locations I'd seen scrawled in the upper left corner of the envelopes that had come before. Mark Madrid, it would seem, was no longer a citizen of Madrid, Spain. Hadn't been for a long time. He had, however, been a resident of such randomly odd locations as Gnaw Bone, Indiana, Slick Lizard, Alabama and Santa Claus, Georgia. This time he'd taken up temporary space on the west coast in a place called Last Chance, Colorado.

GG returned to the kitchen with Johnny Lauten trailing behind her. "It turns out Johnny only had a cup of coffee this morning," she told me while simultaneously pulling out a chair, *her* chair, for our new painter.

"What's up, Chessie?" He straddled the seat as if he were mounting a submissive steed.

"Hey, Johnny." I felt naked in my navy tank top and gray sweat shorts. With Johnny in my kitchen I may as well have been stark naked. He smelled like he'd been stir-fried in deodorant, some Musk scented thing. He took one minute to look into my eyes and then went diving at his huge plate of mushy, lukewarm eggs. GG stood back, her arms folded under her heavy chest. She had a smile on her lips.

"Now, Chessie…you and Johnny and Logan will have to hold the fort down here for a bit. I'll be heading into town."

"Okay, do you need me to bring you?" I asked, delighted in how significant that made me sound.

"No, it's all right. I can grab the bus from up on Main. I could use the exercise."

"Don't be silly, GG. I'll take you over. Where do you have to go?"

Johnny's head was fixed in the down position, gobbling his food as though it was his first and last meal. Johnny Lauten, the perfectly gorgeous, hungry, coffee-drinker painter.

GG leaned into her left hip. "I'm going to pick up some pork chops for tonight." She stared at the envelope still in my fingers.

"It's Colorado now? Last Chance?" I asked.

She drew up her brows and tipped her head toward the top of Johnny's. She was telling me to keep our business to just us. I didn't care if Johnny knew that my would-be father was a rogue world traveler. I didn't care if everybody knew it.

"Well, I guess I should be getting started." Johnny ate faster than anyone I'd ever seen. "That was real good Mrs. B., thank you."

"Of course, and please call me GG." My grandmother would adopt the entire population of Eden's Pond if she could, all 1926 people, or 1927 now, if you included Logan Matthews. Johnny began to take his freshly filled tummy and clean white T-shirt out to the porch, when he stopped and turned around.

"Did you hear what one snowman said to the other? Do you smell carrots?"

I responded with a flimsy chuckle. GG looked completely lost.

"It's a joke, GG. You know—snowmen have carrots for noses," I explained. He waited for it to sink in so she would laugh too. Yet she only offered a polite grin and nod of her head. Johnny was safely outside again when she looked my way.

"Yes, he's a very cute young man," GG said, watching me watch him. "Studying to be a comic, is he? I don't think there's a lot of money in that. He reminds me a little of somebody else I know…somebody I knew once long ago."

I turned the envelope over in my hand. "You mean Mark? Why? Did he tell bad jokes too?"

GG glanced past me and at the window. "That boy has the devil in his details."

"What do you mean?"

"I mean he looks good on the surface, but he's got trouble brewing down deep where you can't see it."

"How can you tell? I think he's kind of sweet, with all the humor. And he has good manners, doesn't he?"

"Manners? Maybe. Sweet? Perhaps. Humor? That's a matter of opinion, my dear. It's what's way down inside that really matters. And Chessie, if there's one thing a woman in her sixtieth year on this earth knows, it's a man who's got the devil in his details. And yes, about your father, I suppose it is Colorado."

Last Chance, to be exact. I wonder if Mark Madrid had chosen that place for a reason, that strange PO Box with such a dramatic name. Was it his last attempt at becoming a father in some way or another? Had the man who'd stolen my mother away from her life outgrown the devil inside him?

★

Johnny Lauten painted with his shirt off. It was only eleven a.m. and 92 sticky degrees. The air conditioner in the living room window chugged along, and I sat between it and the artificial ficus tree so I could gaze outside and not be noticed. He didn't realize I'd been studying his every move but I couldn't get out of my own way quickly enough to prevent Logan from catching me. She'd arrived home with her effortless self, breezing right past our half-naked painter as if he were no more interesting than the wood he was working on. He stopped to say a word or two as she rolled on by. In her true Logan form, she responded with a short smile and an incidental flip of her head. She was putting her plate in the microwave oven, even though GG wasn't home to witness the consumption of her food.

"Is he a good friend of yours?" she asked me.

I had already changed my seat so I couldn't see him. It was enough to know he was there. "You mean Johnny? No, not really."

"He seems nice."

"Yeah, he's very nice looking." And Wish Number Two.

"I said he's nice, not nice looking," she corrected me and sat on the sofa with the dish in her lap, eating without spilling one drop. I keep thinking if she did, GG wouldn't fuss about it, even though she hates it when we eat anyplace other than the kitchen.

"Well, don't you think he's good looking?" I asked.

Logan twisted her mouth in circles, her lips in deliberation. "I don't know. He isn't my type. I guess he's okay… *You* like him though, don't you?"

I suppose it didn't take a rocket scientist to figure that one out. And if Logan could tell, it suddenly dawned on me that maybe Johnny could tell too.

I shrugged her off with a "whatever," and then steered the subject as far away from my obvious feelings for Johnny as I could. "So, do you think you're going to talk to him?"

"Talk to who?"

"To Mark."

Logan took a deep sigh and pushed her last bit of eggs across the plate with the flip side of her fork. "At first I was thinking, no way. My aunt spent months trying to locate him, and he was nowhere to be found. It's like he wants things to exist on his terms only, as if *he* wants to exist on his terms only. But there's this part of me with this insistent need to know what he's got cooking now. That part wants me to say yes. How about you?"

I had only known my half-sister for a short time and already I was able to tell she was a deep thinker. She carried on these powerful debates within her own mind, carefully and logically. I assumed it was all the math training from when she was an Algebra Mathlete. She was staring at me, waiting for my intelligent, well thought out reply, and all I could think about was how Meg went to Doc Abner's this morning because she thought she might have mono and that Johnny had no shirt on. In that instant I was saved by the bell. He rang once and then opened the door a crack, enough to slip his head through. His hair was damp where it joined his face, which had a toasty, reddish glow.

"Hey, listen," Johnny said, "I need another drop cloth, so I'm gonna fly home for a few minutes."

"Okay. Sure, Johnny." I reached up to fumble with my bangs. Logan said nothing at all. She got up, her long, brown legs carrying her into the kitchen where I heard the faucet run. Johnny didn't leave at first. He was certain to keep his eyes on her as she went. And then he turned to me.

"Chess…what do you think she'll say if I ask her out?" He didn't bother with keeping his voice low, and I wasn't sure if he had sweat on his chin, or if he was drooling.

It took me a moment to gather my words, during which time I yanked the knife out of my heart. "I don't know, Johnny. Why don't you try it and see for yourself?" I rose to my feet too, determined to make my own graceful exit.

"Okay, I will. Thanks," he said to the back of my head. I imagined he was staring at me too, the way he did to her, with a gleam in his eye that said the things boys wanted to yet didn't right off the bat. The look of a boy with the devil in his details.

## All the Bad Pumpkins

Meg was talking about cutting her hair. We were at Wong's Chinese Restaurant sharing a plate of vegetable lo mein. It was 3 p.m., and I had to escape my house where Johnny had been working all day. I knew he was waiting for the right time to get Logan alone so he could ask her out, maybe to a movie or for ice cream. Maybe he'd even take her to the Dairy Maid on a night when I was there, and I could serve them their official first date meal.

"I'm thinking of having it cut real short like just past my ears and then I'll wear big hoop earrings all the time. I'll have a pair in every color to match my clothes. What do you think, Chessie?"

"I don't know. I like it long."

Meg kept trying to work the chopsticks while I shot conventional using a plastic fork to collect the greasy brown noodles. I was ruining my dinner appetite but I didn't care. I could get away with skipping meals as much as I wanted to. GG would think it was the Big S striking again.

"Everyone has long hair these days." Including me, including Logan. Still, Meg didn't care. It was more important to her that she be one of a kind. She was happy because she was one of the only girls in town with mono, at least according to Doc Abner. She was supposed to be home resting, but she said she felt "perfectly peachy, doll."

"Your brother's going to ask Logan on a date," I said, sounding a little like a tattletale.

"*Get out!*" Meg shouted, startling a small child sitting in the next booth. "God, he's bad-ass horny," she said with her mouth full. The kid's mother sped a set of dagger eyes our way.

"It doesn't matter. I don't think she'll say yes. She told me he isn't her type."

Meg stabbed a noodle with the tip of the stick. "Not her type? You know what that means, don't you?"

"Not really."

"Logan doesn't like Johnny because he's not black."

"I don't think so, Meg."

"Of course it does. She's a racist."

"She doesn't seem like it. I mean, her own parents were a mixed couple."

"Right, and her dad is white and she hates him." Meg tossed the chopsticks onto the side of the plate, admitting defeat at last.

"I don't think she hates him because he's white. She hates him because he abandoned her. She hates him for the same reason I do."

Meg sat up, tilted her face and gave me a sideways grin. "Sorry, Chess. Sometimes, I kind of forget that. And you've got great hair, by the way. Never cut it."

I stared into her clear blue eyes, thinking about who might become Meg's best friend one year or so from now. I wondered if she would be mad at me, so, so mad for not telling her the truth about my being sick. I wanted to, a thousand times. But Meg's the biggest loudmouth on the planet. She's told every secret I'd ever confided in her—pinky sworn, holy bible irrelevant. There was too much at stake now. Still, I felt like I was cheating on her somehow, like the Big S and I were involved in some sort of lurid affair.

"I'm full." I pushed back into the red leather cushion behind me.

"Me, too. Okay. You pick this time." Meg reached for the fortune cookies, grabbing them both in her left hand.

I eyed the two innocent biscuits. They were not a barometer of the truth or a magic eight ball. They were two fairly tasteless free treats. I lifted one of them, cracked it open and didn't look.

"Me first." Meg slid her paper out in one smooth motion. "It says, 'A tall, dark stranger will make a big impression on you.'"

"Wow. Okay mine says, 'You will lead a long and happy life.'" It was clear Meg and I had probably picked the wrong ones. Hers was meant for me and mine for her.

Logan was the tall, dark stranger. And Meg's life was surely going to be long and happy.

"Cool," she said with a shrug. "I'd like to meet a new guy. Maybe a black one. Does Logan have a brother?"

I gave her a playful shove and quietly tucked the fortune into the front pocket of my shorts.

✳

Logan and GG were playing cards when I arrived back home—crazy eights, and Logan was winning. "Can we deal you in?" GG asked. There were tiny beads of sweat on her upper lip atop a five o-clock shadow she put peroxide on once a week.

"No, I'm going to hop in the shower." I smiled at the two of them, secretly wondering whether Logan was Johnny's new girl-friend now.

I felt instantly relieved as the water rushed through the length of my hair. It was right then when it occurred to me that Mark Madrid was out there in Last Chance waiting for me to absolve his sins. Perhaps it was high time for me to give the devil his due.

✳

"I'll talk to him," I said the next morning while GG and I folded the clean, dry towels from the laundry basket. Logan was still in the bathroom. I figured I'd be the first one to tell her, beat Logan to the punch.

GG pushed her glasses up on the bridge of her nose and an-gled her head to look at me. "To your father?"

"Yes, to Mark. I'll listen to what he has to say," I announced.

She snapped a towel out in front of her. "Okay, then you've both agreed."

"Who both?"

"You and Logan have both agreed. She told me late last night."

"Fine…so when? What are we supposed to do, call him up or what?"

"No, I'll make the arrangements for him to contact you two," she said being all Ghita Barraco, secret agent for the FBI.

Just then a car door slammed. Johnny arrived, forty minutes late, but he was here. GG hadn't bothered to save any breakfast. She despised tardiness. "There's never a reason that's good enough," she would say.

Johnny fumbled over his excuse, saying he'd overslept and then run low on gas and had to stop at a station to fill up. She was right. He sounded lame, at least his words sounded lame and as he turned to head out without an offering of GG's food, I felt a little sorry for him. Twenty minutes later, Logan rushed past me on her way outside, smelling of soap and baby powder, her hair gathered up in a ponytail which was still damp.

"Where are you going?" I asked.

"For a walk. Wanna come?"

It was an overcast morning. Raindrops loomed out there somewhere, however they were graciously late too.

"We need a plan," she said.

"A plan?"

"Yes. If we're going to talk to our father then we'll need to have a plan."

I had no idea why we needed to plan a conversation, though Logan seemed so convinced that I said I'd go with her figuring maybe she knew something important that I didn't. She and I took our steps together right past Johnny's leering glances and out the front gate. We weren't ten feet past the house when she burst into her words.

"I don't know if I can forgive him. I don't know if too much time has passed. Do you think you can?"

"I don't know either. Probably not. I think I want to scream at him." I never said that to anybody before, and it suddenly felt safe to admit.

"Me too. Although I think if we attack him straight out then we won't get the chance to say much else."

The only thing I wanted to say to Mark Madrid was that he was a fool for ever leaving my mother for hers. I wanted to ask him what Janet Matthews had that Mom didn't. Was it the lure of her race? The attraction to something so completely different from himself? Did Mark cheat because he was a womanizer as GG said or because of one woman in particular? Was he like Johnny Lauten who seemed so intrigued with Logan that he could barely keep the paint off himself? Maybe Johnny had a secret desire to sleep with a girl unlike any other he'd ever been with. Maybe my father did too.

I didn't notice that Logan had still been talking without taking a breath. What I did notice was an old Chevy pickup truck driving slowly past us. I knew exactly who it was. His name was Cole Harris and he was in my graduating class, even though he was three years older than me. He was left back more than one time on account of being a little slow, which people say is on account of his parents being first cousins. Nobody liked Cole. Even the grown-ups had a hard time liking him. He composed raunchy poetry, licked rocks, and had a pet snake he slept with. He pulled down his window as he slowed his truck to a crawl.

"Chessie. Chessie Madrid," he spoke out. He had a whistle in his S since he was missing a bottom tooth, front and center and a deep southern drawl as if he'd come from the backwoods of Alabama.

I ignored him and Logan nudged me as if I hadn't heard.

"Yeah, hey Cole," I said and kept on walking.

"Chessie Madrid, who's that you got with you there?"

"I'll be right there, Logan." I left her to head over to him. "What do you want, Cole?"

"Is that your brand new sister?"

I tried to control the volume of his voice with my own. "Yes," I said softly.

"Is she a nigger or what? I heard she's a nigger. She don't look all that black to me."

I swung my head around to check on her, to be sure she hadn't heard. Her face was down, her eyes keeping contact with the flat even stones in the roadway.

"You're an idiot Cole, you know that?" I hissed.

"So if she's a nigger and she's your sister, does that make you one too?" He was grinning a stupid, toothless grin like a mean old jack-o-lantern.

"She's my half-sister if you really must know!"

"So you're just a half nigger!" Cole laughed, and I saw clear down his throat to his tonsils.

"And you're a giant asshole!" I turned again to peek at her. That's when I realized she had taken off running down the street with her long, graceful legs carrying her away. I only called after her once. I knew she wouldn't wait up for me no matter how many times I called.

"She runs like one though. Ain't them people quick, huh?"

All at once my fist had a mind of its own. It rocketed through the car window, landing smack dab in the middle of that ugly pumpkin face. His neck snapped back, his eyes big and round. "You're a waste of life Cole Harris, you know that? They ought to keep you locked up in some dark cellar with your snakes and your rocks! Go to hell. Go straight to hell!"

I walked home by myself with random thoughts like logs on a fire, sparking and crackling loudly in my mind. Infidelity. Racism. Love and hate. Maybe I should have wished for a puppy. Boys. Girls. Boys and girls. Life and death. Maybe I had wished Logan and Mark into my life. If so, was Johnny going to fall for me anytime soon?

I rounded the corner to my house as though I was on autopilot and was inside even before Logan. I smiled at Johnny as he winked my way. I smiled in spite of my better judgment. The logs in my head were burning up. Who was I if I wasn't pleasing Johnny? Who was I when I raged at Cole?

★

Six hours passed. Logan refused dinner spending the majority of the night in her room talking on the telephone.

"Do you suppose she's missing her family?" GG asked from behind her needlepoint loom.

"I know I'd be missing mine if I were her." I looked down the hallway to the face of her door.

"Maybe you could see if she's all right."

I stepped quietly until I reached the door, tapping my fingers against the hollow wood frame.

She didn't say anything, just turned the knob and stood there looking at me.

"Can I come in?" What I really wanted to say was more than I wanted GG to overhear.

"Sure." Logan moved aside for me as I entered and then closed myself in.

"Look, I really want to apologize for this morning, for that boy and what he said. He's like mentally challenged or something… everybody around here knows that about him."

"It's okay. I don't care about him." If she were to finish her sentence she would have said it was me and my words that hurt her more. I had all but disowned her, and she knew it as well as I did.

"Well, we still have to finish making that plan." I was talking to the back of her as she walked over to the bed to grab a hold of the phone receiver.

"It's kind of silly. I guess we don't really need a plan." She was facing me again, taking me in with a dull, flat stare.

"No, we do, we do need a plan…maybe tomorrow we can figure it all out."

"Yeah, maybe," she said and then forced a grin I imagined was killing her.

✦

Doc Abner rifled through the pages inside a brown folder, an inch or so thick, all about me. Outside the sky was dark, and spitting spiky raindrops. Inside his office three fluorescent bulbs washed the ceiling in a pasty gray light. I had on a paper nightgown with a paper belt and I crunched each time I shifted position.

Doc's hair had a fresh layer of black shoe polish on it, all glossy and teased in place. I tried not to stare directly at it, like it was a solar eclipse and I was in danger of going blind. A little picture frame on his desk held a photo of Mrs. Abner, all dressed up in a yellow pantsuit and wearing a matching hat with a big yellow feather on top. I wondered if he loved her, if he ever cheated on her, or if he ever wanted to. Maybe he even had a thing for GG.

He cleared a pocket of phlegm from his throat. "How are you feeling?"

"Okay except for the episodes."

His eyes fell gently on mine. "Are they coming more frequently?"

"Three or four a week now." I kicked the rear end of my sandal with the front of the other one. The inside of my mouth tasted like I'd eaten scrap metal.

"So that would be a yes?"

"I guess so."

He scribbled something. Perhaps he was making a wish list too. Perhaps I was on it.

"Francesca, there's a specialist in St. Louis I'd like you to see. I spoke to him about your case and he's interested in you. I think your grandmother agrees."

"I hear they have good Chinese food in St. Louis." I suspected it wasn't the response he was looking for. "When?"

"Over the next few weeks. I can make the arrangements for you, if you like."

"I have to talk to GG about it first."

Doc Abner had two crescent moons of sweat under his arms, evident through his thin blue shirt. He wasn't wearing his doctor jacket or his stethoscope. I began to consider that he wasn't a real MD at all. He seemed more uptight than usual so I figured I'd forgo the ritualistic busting of chops. I allowed him to see me off with a polite pat on my back. He knew my mother, once said I looked exactly like her.

The rain picked up, got steadily more intense as the day wore on. I spent most of it in bed, willing her to come to me again.

"Mama? Where have you been? I need to talk to you. Logan's here. I assume you probably know all about her. Are you mad? I really hope not. She's pretty nice. I'm afraid I wished her here… Mama?"

From downstairs I heard GG and Logan talking.

"Is Chessie okay?" Logan asked.

"She's just tired. She'll be fine by tomorrow." I fell asleep loving the sound of my grandmother's lies.

# Gracious Love

I was with Meg as she did her version of multi-tasking, chewing bubble gum while simultaneously smoking a cigarette. I'd been there for an hour and still hadn't mentioned anything about how I hurt Logan even though I didn't mean to, and how I punched Cole Harris in the face. I think she'd be happy about that part since she hated Cole Harris ever since he put white paste in her milk carton in elementary school.

"Okay, so I really have to figure out who I got mono from," she was saying as she grabbed a tiny notepad with purple hearts on the cover. She was in the middle of her bed, her legs strewn apart and bent at the knee. Emerson the cat crawled slowly in the empty space between her thighs.

"You might need more paper then. And *she's* getting so fat," I said, referring to the kitty she'd had for almost three years. Johnny found her behind the shed in their yard, all matted gray fur and bulging bones.

She took a pen in her other hand, the one without the cigarette in it. "It's Johnny's fault. He overfeeds her. Besides, when you're a cat you don't have to worry about your waistline, right? Anyhow, let's see, I made out with Dan Ritter at Missy Trunk's graduation party. Then there was Elliott somebody or other that I met at the mall, he works at the food court. OH! Damn! I'll bet it was Paul Caprice. He said he had a sore throat the night at Shelley's." Meg smashed the butt out in a heart-shaped ashtray on her nightstand.

"Really, Meg, you ought to be careful kissing so many different guys."

"Why? It's mad fun and besides, you live like a nun, Chessie. And you're real pretty. We have to get you hooked up with somebody. Who do you think about when the lights go out at night? Who is it that curls your toes? Come on, spill it!"

As if on cue, Johnny, my painter and toe-curler, appeared in the doorway wearing his sweetest smile. "Whatcha girls up to tonight?"

"What does it look like?" Meg snapped.

"Hey Johnny," I said. I decided to forgive him for wanting to ask Logan out. *Almost* everyone deserves a second shot.

"Hey, Chess."

"Logan isn't here, Johnny, so you can stop poking around." Meg ran her hand over the length of Emerson's tail.

"I'm not looking for her. I was wondering if you guys wanted me to pick you up some beer. I'm heading out to the Kwik Stop for some." He crossed the room, reached into Meg's lap and picked up the cat, with one sturdy hand. "Here you are, Emmy. Slumming with the ladies tonight huh?"

Meg looked at me. "Whadya think?"

"Do you feel up to drinking beer?" I asked.

"Oh hell, yeah. What else is there to do? Okay, we're in."

Johnny leaned into the wall, and stared straight at me. "Cool, 'cause I need a lift. My car is out of gas."

Meg stood up and flung her pen at him. "So you pretend to care when you really just need a ride!"

"That's okay, Meg. I'll take him." Inside I was sure that Johnny was up to something. Yet he was caressing that fat cat with such tenderness that all at once I wanted to be Emerson.

"Deep," he said but I think he meant to say thanks.

"Are you sure, Chessie? You don't have to." Meg took Emerson and gave Johnny a look of disgust.

"I'm sure."

"Hey, smoking will kill you," he remarked, to his sister before sneaking a few out of her pack.

You would think he would've followed me out to my car. Instead, I followed him. He waited until we were inside to light up, and then he cranked the window handle to let out the smoke. I couldn't think of one single thing to say, so I was thankful when he opened his mouth.

"Your grandmother's pretty cool."

The back of my throat felt like sandpaper, and I nodded for fear I had suddenly lost my voice.

"Was she pissed off at me this morning for being late?"

"Um, no, I don't think so."

We didn't speak again until after we arrived at the store. That's when he asked if I was coming in with him. I said no so I could enjoy the view as he walked inside where the ceiling of brilliant white lights were shining just for him, his own private stage. His skin was tanned and his hair golden streaked. His light green shirt was tight around the muscles in his upper arms. I realized I wanted him so much it scared me, since GG's words kept blaring in my head. If Johnny was a devil in disguise, he sure wore his costume well. He told three dirty jokes on the way to Meg's, and all I could think was that I was sad to have our little road trip come to an end. As we turned onto their street, Johnny reached across to touch the radio dial and made direct contact with my bare knee.

"Hey, you in any hurry to get back?" he asked.

"I don't think so."

"Good. Pull over and switch places with me," he ordered and I did. I had no idea at all what he was thinking, and I didn't care. He wanted to be with me, not Logan or anyone else at the moment. Me. As I got into the passenger seat and he adjusted the one I'd turned over to him, he glanced my way. His gaze slid from the top of my head and seemed to get caught somewhere between there and my waist. If I wasn't mistaken, he was staring at my chest, my barely 32 B's which I prayed would impress him with their perkiness since their size was somewhat lacking. I straightened my spine for insurance.

"Where are we going?" I managed to inquire.

"I need to run over to a friend's and pick something up." Even though he was driving, he popped open a beer and took a long swig. "So what's your deal, Chessie? You got a boyfriend or what?"

"Not right now."

"Why is that? I mean, you *do* like guys, don't you?"

"Of course!" And there it was. Johnny Lauten hadn't fallen in love with me yet because he thought I might be a lesbian. I wasn't sure if I was completely insulted or completely relieved. Maybe that's why he wanted to ask Logan out instead of me. "I was seeing somebody earlier this year. But it didn't work out," I lied.

Johnny pulled over in front of a small dark bungalow and put the car in park. "That's too bad. I'll bet you'd be a gracious lover." Then without another word he jumped out and rushed to the door of the house. I watched as he was met there by a lady who looked way older than me or him. They exchanged words and she handed him an envelope, which he slipped into his back pocket. He then accepted a hug from whoever she was, and though I wouldn't swear to it, she may have smacked him on the ass. I saw Meg, in my mind's eye, standing at the window of her room cursing her dumb-as-a-stump brother for taking me away. In a minute he was with me again and staring my way. There was this weird look on his face.

"You feel like getting high?" He settled into the seat, his legs falling apart at the knees. He wasn't driving, just sitting there with that look.

I only smoked pot once before at a party; it made me see things that weren't really there. Meg got so stoned one time that she drove her father's brand new Buick through the carwash with the windows rolled down. The inside of my head was jam packed with No's flying all over the place.

"Okay," I said defying the real me for some willing imposter. Hanging out with him was suddenly extremely important. Johnny drove my car to the end of the road where there wasn't much aside from some old dead trees and the hollowed out carcass of a station wagon that looked like it had once been on fire.

We didn't talk. He gave me a can of beer and lit up the joint that came out of the envelope the touchy feely lady gave him. I was immediately sick from the smell of the smoke in the air even before he passed it to me. I tried my best to remember how to do it so that I didn't look naïve or inexperienced or uncool. Impressing him became my one objective. I turned into the girl he needed me to be; agreeable, easy. And by the way, what did he mean by a gracious lover anyway?

Johnny let me drive to his house. He was resting in the passenger seat with a placid, glazed expression. I could appreciate his gentle side, even if nobody else could.

"Pull up a little," he said, instructing me to move past his front door and beyond the row of boxwood hedges on the edge of their lawn. My face was down when he took it, with just one hand under my chin, lifting my head so I was looking at him. Things were moving in super slow motion as he came toward me, placing his mouth on mine. He kept his tongue to himself. He left me with a small, dry kiss from lips that tasted like Budweiser.

I was dizzy, spinning from the inside out. I felt like I swallowed a hundred butterflies. It was all I could to keep from floating up and away.

✳

Two days went by since the night of Johnny and me. I pretended we were in a secret affair since he'd come over to finish painting, and hadn't done more than smile at me once or twice. He smiled at Logan too, which I assumed was to keep things looking normal on the outside. I kept trying to line up some time alone with him, discreetly of course, but so far it hadn't happened. This morning he announced to GG that he'd be wrapping up the entire job by day's end tomorrow. A surge of panic shot through me, as if that meant I might never see him again, and our affair would end before it had a real chance to begin.

I didn't tell Meg that her brother and I had our own little party or that we had our second kiss, if you count the one in the closet so long ago. I knew she'd have something to say like, "Lost your marbles have you, Chess? Don't you see how pathetic he is?" To which I'd have to say, yeah, I guess, sort of, sometimes, and I'd plead guilty by reason of temporary romantic insanity.

I was pretty sure everything was okay with Logan and me. She never mentioned Cole Harris or missing her friends back home again. She kept running as if she were on a mission. Maybe it was to run all the way to Louisiana one day when we least expect it. Just after she got in today, GG sat us down on the sofa and stood before us, all official, her body taut and at attention.

"I've been in touch with your father. He's planning to contact you girls very soon." She was wearing her yellow housecoat, the one that makes her skin look see-through.

About fifteen minutes later when the telephone rang, Logan and I exchanged a brief panicked look. After all, we hadn't even devised our plan of action yet. I would have to go with my original idea—tell him what a jerk he was for leaving my mom, tell him he missed out on a life with a terrific lady and a terrific daughter too, if I said so myself. But it turned out to be my boss from the Dairy Maid asking if I could fill in for George at work tonight. "He's sick," he told me. I didn't want to do it, especially for George and his stupid sickness. Ever since the Big S I had little patience for people with their upper respiratory infections or their stomach flues. Even Meg with her dopey mono. Part of me relished that I could be pretend-well. Yet another part of me wanted to scream out, "Oh you think *you're* sick, huh?" I agreed to work though because you never knew when you'd need a favor from somebody in return.

★

The store was technical mayhem. I spilled an entire gallon of melted chocolate ice cream down the front of my uniform and burnt my finger on the deep fryer. To make matters worse, my boss asked if I could bring George his paycheck since he wouldn't be in for the rest of the week.

"Why, what's wrong with him?" I asked, and it was Patty, the other Dairy Maid maid that answered.

"I think he got beat up."

I was running my finger under a cool tap. "He did? You're kidding. George was in a fight?"

"Yup. Poor George."

Maybe it was morbid curiosity that made me agree to go to his house with his paycheck. Partly I didn't believe that anyone would bother beating up a kid like George, a kid who seemed like he wouldn't squish an ant even by accident. When he answered the door, he had his hair combed all the way down over his right eye yet I could see where his skin went purple underneath. He had red streak marks across his left check and a puffy top lip. Patty was right. Poor George.

"Hi."

"Hi, Chessie. Thanks for coming." He made direct eye contact with me with his one good eye.

"Are you all right?"

"Yeah, sure." He had on a grey sweatshirt with sleeves that were cut off at the elbow. It was like 500 degrees outside, and I wondered if he realized it.

"What happened? Who did this to you?"

"Look, it doesn't make a difference. I appreciate your bringing me my money." He held out his hand for the envelope that I still had in mine.

"Okay, well, I'm sorry." I handed it over.

"Why? You didn't do it."

"That's what people say when they feel badly for someone else," I informed him, straining to contain the faintest hint of impatience.

"Oh, thanks."

I left before he could thank me again. His gratitude made me uncomfortable. And it made me think about Johnny, and how he said I was a gracious lover right before he put his mouth on mine.

I drove through the streets of Edenville at 10:45 with a sticky blouse and a throbbing pointer finger when I spotted a group of kids hanging out in a gas station parking lot. Nothing new, a typical scene, bunch of locals with no agenda. Looked quick. Looked away. Looked again. It was Johnny, sitting up on the roof of a car. His legs were splayed and a girl I didn't know lounged in between them. A big brown bag was open on the ground, which was where I assumed the case of beer was being stored. I wanted to move out of sight before he noticed me, but I was trapped at a red light that glared at me, torturing and taunting—"you're stuck here—now what?" I wanted to watch and not watch both at once. Why was my Wish Number Two sitting so close to that other girl? And why was his arm hung over her shoulder, his hand dangling in front of her chest? She passed him a cigarette, but not until after she had it in her mouth. Then I knew they were getting high, like we did on our first date since seven minutes in heaven. The traffic signal turned green then, and I did too, as Johnny leaned in, his face inches from hers—one inch, maybe no inch.

I wanted to cry. More than that, I wanted to be angry. I didn't want to have to concede to Meg, even in my mind, about her brother being pathetic. Maybe he was waiting for me to say thank you, the way George had done again and again. Perhaps he was sorry for me, or perhaps he was waiting for something more than a kiss. I wiped two pushy tears off my cheeks.

I took a look down at myself as I arrived home, hoping GG had already gone to bed. I opened the door to find the living room dark except for the white and gray shadows the TV screen sent flickering through the air. And there was Logan, sitting straight up in the corner chair, facing me. Her skin looked drained of all its natural color. Her eyes were rimmed in red.

"What is it? What's wrong?" I asked.

"He called. Mark called."

Suddenly Logan, strong and steady Logan, looked as though she was ready to lunge out of the chair and sprint from here to someplace else, anyplace else. What could he have said to make her this way? Whatever it was, I was surely his next victim. If nothing else, my mood had quickly shifted. Now, I was angry.

# A Pebble in Your Shoe

"You can't paint in the rain," GG was saying. She bustled around the kitchen like a dizzy, spinning top, stopping only long enough to glance out the window at the puddles that kept Johnny from our porch that next morning. She seemed all jittery and completely unaware she was wearing two different earrings—one that looked like a gold teardrop and another, a small silver ball. Poor GG hadn't even matched up the colors. She had on her powder blue seersucker dress and kept tugging at the cinched waistband. I decided my grandmother was literally coming undone at the seams since her hem was falling at the back of her knee. I thought it might have been worry making her behave that way, worry for me, worry for herself if the Big S got the better of me.

"We should make that trip to St. Louis," she had said, a firm suggestion wrapped in a soft request.

"I guess." It was the best I could do. I kept thinking about Logan and what we'd tell her as to why we were leaving for a little excursion out of town. Logan had become a distraction. With her here I thought less and less about dying and more and more about family and sisterhood and dreams that could possibly come true. I was just beginning to feel comfortable with her, especially after last night when we went up to my room where I put a blanket over the heating vent and we whispered into the late hours about Mark Madrid and what he said and didn't say.

It was shortly after I got home and found Logan looking about as raggedy as Ann that I invited her upstairs for the first time since she came to Eden's Pond. When we got there, she plopped in the middle of my floor, hugged her knees and shook her head. "I don't know. It was so weird."

"Go on," I instructed as I peeled off my damp and sticky uniform shirt, not bothering to turn around. It didn't matter anyway. She was staring off at a spot on my wall so intently that I looked behind me to be sure nothing was there.

"Well, to begin with, he sounds a lot like my math teacher which was confusing on some level. Anyhow, I think he was nervous, because he cleared his throat over and over."

"Maybe he has a cold," I suggested and then felt stupid for saying so.

"I don't know. For the first few minutes we made small talk, well—*he* did mostly. He asked about school and my plans for the future and if I drove a car yet. I answered like I was filling in the blanks in some weird survey."

"Did you ask him any questions?"

She rested her chin on the top of her bent leg. "Not right away. After he was finished with the general topic of me, he started rambling on about how he's involved in a project to save the polar bears in Alaska. He must have gone on for ten minutes about the polar bears."

"Polar bears? He's saving polar bears in Alaska?" I pulled a clean tank top over my head and tried to envision Mark Madrid in a parka changing his name to Mark Anchorage.

"He's planning to. It was like he didn't know what else to say. That's when I got up the courage to ask why he wanted to speak to me now."

I sat on the floor across from her, leaning against my box frame. "You did? What did he say?"

"He said that too much time had passed too quickly, and he was thinking it might be good to catch up."

"To catch up? God, it's like he thinks we're old friends of his!"

"Well, I don't know what we are. We live on the same planet and share DNA, but we have no connection. He's a stranger. He never even asked about my mom or said he was sorry for anything. He was just cordial and casual and neat."

Logan described the man I remembered, the man who placed drama in the oddest places and never where it deserved to be. She described the man who my mother adored for his even temperament and his ability to under-react.

"Is he married now?" I asked.

"I didn't want to know. He said "we" a few times as in 'We're taking a trip to Washington this winter.' I was scared there was another family out there—one he didn't leave."

"I hate him," I whispered, "I really hate him." It felt good to say that out loud, even if I hadn't shouted it from the rooftop. I had never admitted it before, not even to GG or Meg. I pretended to be well adjusted in spite of him.

"But what good does it do—hating him? I mean, I want to hate him too. I think we have a right to. But what will it solve?"

"I don't know," I sighed. It had been a rough night. I was really tired, and I needed a shower. I lost my almost new boyfriend to another woman and someone beat up George, whose swollen face I kept seeing whenever I closed my eyes. Sometimes you needed to hate somebody. Sometimes you needed a place to dump all the bad things you carried around after they got so heavy you could hardly stand. Maybe that's what hating Mark would solve. "I don't know," I said again, throwing my head against the bed.

Logan stood up. "My mother used to say that hatred is like a pebble stuck in your shoe. It hurts until you get it out, and if you keep walking around with it there you'll end up crippled."

I wanted to come back with something inspirational my mother left me with, yet the only thing I could think of was "never talk with food in your mouth" which didn't seem to fit the mood. "So you can forgive him then?" I asked.

She stretched her arms over her head and then out at her sides. "Back home, at our church, Pastor Clark preaches about forgiveness. He says it's the way of Jesus."

"It's not that easy," I said.

Logan had her very own pastor. I didn't go to church much. GG said it was up to me and never pushed when I didn't feel like it, which was on most Sundays.

"Anyway, he wants to see me, but he says it's my choice. I told him I guess it'd be okay. So I think you'll have to figure out whether you can find a way to move past your hatred since I'm sure he'll want to see you too."

"Did he say he was planning to come here? Did he say he was coming to Eden's Pond?" I stood up only long enough to fall down into the row of throw pillows stacked on my bed.

"No. He said that he'd like it if we could get together. You don't suppose he expects us to go all the way out to Colorado, do you?"

"Well if he does, I'm not going. If he wants to see me that badly he knows where to find me." Decision number one, down.

Logan rolled her head around in circles as though it was in danger of falling off the top of her neck and needed tightening. "Yeah, I don't see a reason to run to him just because he called."

So Mark's two daughters were on the same page. We sat together on my bed and carried on talking until the grandfather clock in the downstairs hallway announced the arrival of one a.m. I forgot Logan wasn't somebody I'd known my whole life. I forgot she was the reminder of Mark's raging infidelity. In the ordinary occurrence of one day becoming the next, I found out Logan had a boyfriend named Anthony she broke up with after he slapped her in the face. I found out she liked to bowl and loved live music, especially this jazz guy I never heard of, Harry somebody. We both eat peanut butter on bananas and we're both allergic to pineapple. I wouldn't go as far as to say that I made a sister last night, however at the very least I may have made a friend.

✯

I was grateful for another day of rain, grateful Johnny wasn't around with his paint splattered jeans, his one-liners and his smile. I spent the hour after GG left for town trying to decide how I felt about him. I was able to forgive his interest in Logan since I never saw him sucking the air out of her. I didn't know what made me think he and I had something special. Maybe merely wanting something so badly made it true.

It was ten minutes before noon and I was in the middle of deciphering why I'd been hanging around waiting for Mark's call. I think I was terrified that since he'd spoken to one daughter he had satisfied his urge for parenting for the week. It was one thing to be rejected by him once in a lifetime, but twice is another thing all together. Meg was begging me to come over and watch some movie with her since it was too crummy to hang outside today. Part of me wanted to go and the other part was afraid to. What if Johnny was there, or worse—what if Johnny and the new girl were there?

Logan was in her room writing a letter. I assumed it was for her aunt in jail. I still didn't know exactly what happened to that woman. I almost ventured to ask last night while we were up in my room, but it felt like too much, too soon. GG had gone to town by bus again. It seemed she'd suddenly become quite the fan of public transportation. So it was just me and the telephone, which didn't ring in spite of my staring at it and willing it to do so. If I sat there much longer, I thought I'd probably go insane. I slipped on my sandals and grabbed my keys.

"Logan, I'll see you later. I'm going over to Meg's!" I yelled down the hallway.

"Okay," she replied from behind her door.

I wanted to ask her to call me if she heard from Mark again. Yet I was already rushing to my car, dodging the raindrops and thinking that I didn't always need to be so available.

☆

Meg had moved to Eden's Pond one year before my mother died. We weren't friends, straight away. I had no experience with girls who weren't always the same, one day to the next. And Meg was personality du jour. Mom had this way of knowing, in the first five minutes, whether somebody was good or bad, not for herself, but for me. In the blink of an intuitive eye, at the beginning of Meg and me, my mother had formed an opinion. "Chess," she said, "this girl's imperfect, and imperfect people make the most perfect friends. It's a lot easier to be human around them." After the accident, in the months right after Mom was gone, with the contents of my world all topsy-turvy, I was nice and mean, scared and certain. I was ugly, pretty, thin and fat and through it all, Meg was there, as constant as if she weren't human, if only long enough for me to find my feet and then find the ground again.

When I got to Meg's, she fell asleep a half an hour after I arrived, in the middle of my talking, mid-sentence, leaving me sitting there watching some stupid movie where a guy kept killing people with a chainsaw. I was annoyed but not all that much. I just covered her with a quilt, and tiptoed down the stairs. That's when I saw him. It was too late to turn around. He was lying on the couch awake, with Emerson purring on his chest.

"What's up, Chessie?"

"Hey, Johnny…Meg's sleeping, so can you tell her that I'll talk to her tonight?"

"You leaving?"

"Yeah."

"So soon? That's too bad…" He pushed his body against the back of the sofa and twisted around to face me. "Why don't you sit here with me for a while?"

I turned off that part of my brain that invited reason, as I took a seat across from him on the wing-backed chair that Meg's mom usually reads in. Her parents were never home anymore since they opened their shop in Edenville—handcrafted wood furniture and odds and ends GG said were way too pricey for folks in this area.

"I got some more of that pot from the other night down in my room. You feel like smoking with me?" After he was finished with college Johnny moved into the basement for more privacy. Meg said it was better that way because she didn't have to see him as much.

"No, I really have to get going. Maybe some other time."

"Oh, come on. It's no fun to party all alone."

"All right—I guess so." I was a helpless, mindless clod as I trailed him down the steps and into his bedroom, which was dark and even messier than Meg's. There was only one window, with a piece of cut cardboard in front of it to block the light. There was no place to sit except for his bed where the sheets were all knotted up and half hanging on the floor. I stayed on my clod legs as he sat there, opening a small plastic bag and removing a joint, a grin and a wink.

"You gonna stay way over there?" he asked.

"I don't know."

"It's okay. I won't bite."

I hesitated as I was sure I heard footsteps above. Emerson, I thought. Hopefully Emerson and not Meg. "No, um…listen Johnny, I shouldn't. I mean, I really don't even usually do this all that much."

Just then he lit a match and burst into laughter. "Of course you don't. You're a baby. I know that. But there's nothing wrong with that, Chessie. There's nothing wrong with being a baby."

I could feel my cheeks filling up like they do when I'm either mad or embarrassed or both, which was the case as Johnny looked over at me. "I'm *not* a baby."

"Yeah, ya are. It's okay. It's kinda cute."

"I saw you last night—in Edenville. I saw you at the gas station." I didn't know where I was going with this or why.

"And?"

"And you were with some girl."

"And?"

"Is she your girlfriend?"

He was laughing again. "Sweetie, I don't even remember her name."

"I have to go." I turned on my heel. He leaped off the bed and reached for my arm, which he caught without a hitch. He pulled me over to him and pressed me into the brown paneled wall. His lips were on mine again and this time he pushed his tongue into my mouth without being invited. His breath was stale as week-old gym shorts and it made me want to gag. I pushed him off with one heated shove.

"You don't do that, Johnny. You don't kiss a person that way."

He laughed again, and I took off up the stairs as quickly as my feet would allow. Even though I was wearing sandals, it felt as if there was a huge pebble caught in my shoe, beneath my big toe.

☆

I thought about love for the rest of the day. I kept wondering how men behaved when they fell in love. Did they lose critical brain cells, think with their penis'? Forget their manners? Hurl hurtful insults through the air? If so, then maybe Wish Number Two was really happening. I thought to raise the subject over dinner, maybe ask GG or Logan in a hypothetical way so as not to arouse suspicion.

Then I thought twice. Men would remain a mystery, at least for what was left of the evening. Even Mark Madrid was bugging me. There'd been no other calls from him today while I was gone, and the phone didn't ring once until Meg called to apologize for falling asleep.

At ten p.m. I changed into my pajamas and fell into bed. I was nearly at the point of drifting off, at that place where you leave reality behind and rush into your waiting dreams, when I heard the noise below. GG was at the foot of the stairs calling to me.

"Chessie! Chessie, are you still up?"

I appeared at my door in an instant. "What is it GG? What's wrong?"

"It's the phone, it's your father."

My heart took off racing down the steps ahead of me. Easy Chessie. You hate him, remember?

"Okay, I'll be right there," I said as calmly as I could.

This was it. The chance to speak my mind or at least give Mark Madrid a piece of it. I coached myself along the way. Don't blow it. Don't cave and, more than that, don't be a baby.

GG held the receiver in the small space between us. Her eyes were checking mine as she gave my shoulder a firm squeeze before leaving the room.

I figured I could hang up, without a word. That might say everything I should have said to the man who left me so long ago. I stared at the telephone in my hand and then brought it slowly to my face.

"Hello."

## Those Three Little Words

Certain moments can freeze time, literally make it stop dead in its tracks. Taking a phone call from a father you haven't spoken to in over ten years is one of those moments. The air was warm in the house and the palm of my hand was damp, so the receiver slid in my grip. I heard myself say hello and waited for what felt like forever to hear the reply.

"Francie…it's me. It's—"

"I know who it is." Mark Madrid was the only person in the whole world who ever called me Francie. It was my mom who got Chessie from Francesca. I think he felt as if he needed to come up with something all his own to compete with her. I didn't like it much then—even less now.

"How are you, Francie? It's so good to hear your voice."

"I'm fine, and I'm not Francie."

"Oh, that's right. It's Chessie, isn't it?"

"Yes."

"Do you know where it came from—the nickname Francie?"

"No."

"You were about two-and-a-half and your mom bought you one of those trunks full of dress up clothes. You loved the real fancy ones, the ones with the sparkles and feathers and beads. One day you came prancing in to me saying, "Look at me Daddy, I'm fancy." So I said, "Yes you're fancy Francie. You got such a kick out of that."

"I don't dress up anymore. I'm pretty plain now. Not that

you would know either way, from way out there in runaway father land."

He sidestepped my jab and carried on, unharmed. "I doubt you could ever be plain."

"So I hear you're into bears now…polar bears, is it?"

"Oh, did Logan mention that? Yes. It's an awful situation. They're in danger of extinction."

"That's too bad." I flipped my hair back and tried to sound genuine, not sure if it worked. I had nothing against polar bears but, well, give me a break. Mark Madrid saving something other than himself? It was laughable.

"You've finished high school now, huh?" I don't know what Logan's math teacher sounded like, but my father's voice was raspy and deeper than I remembered, like he'd been yelling a lot recently and didn't have a lozenge.

"Yes, I graduated."

"So you'll be heading off to college soon."

"No, I can't, I mean, maybe. I don't know."

"Wouldn't you like to experience what it's like to go away to school, live in a dorm with a bunch of other girls your age?"

"No."

"Well, it's not for everyone… Listen Chessie, did Logan also mention that I was hoping for a chance to see you girls?"

"She did."

"There's no pressure. I just hope you'll consider it. It's been such a long time and—"

"It's been a *very* long time, Mark."

That's when I heard him draw in his breath. "I don't suppose you could find it in your heart to call me Dad."

"Why would I want to do that?"

He didn't answer, almost for a full minute, and I thought he'd hung up. I was scared that he had. I wanted to be mean, and I also wanted him to take it—whatever it was I needed to spew his way. He should take it like a man. It was the least he could do.

"Okay that's fine, Chessie. Your grandmother knows where

to reach me. Once you've made a decision you can have her be in touch, and we'll set something up."

"I'm not coming to Colorado."

"I don't expect you to. I'd arrange to come to Missouri."

There was a pause, a silence so loud I heard GG rinsing her teeth in the bathroom and the hum of the clock radio beside her bed.

"All right. Well, thank you, Chessie. It's been wonderful hearing your voice. You sound like quite a young woman now. I'll bet you even have a boyfriend."

"Yes. His name is Johnny and he's fantastic. He's loyal."

"That's good. Make sure he treats you right."

"I don't need any dating advice from you. I've got it covered." I was on a mission to induce pain. Nothing was off limits, including lies.

"I hope to hear from you soon. Goodbye."

And just like that, it was over. I went to bed hearing the conversation everywhere, in my curtains and sheets, in my sock drawer, in the rafters above my head. I was unable to escape it. I even heard it in my dreams. I saw him there too, with his long hair still gathered in a ponytail, only now he was missing the top part. Now he had crinkles at the corners of his eyes and his hands had bumpy veins and brown blotches. I realized I had dreamt my father to be much older than he actually was, and in reality he might not look all that different than he did fifteen years ago. Then I realized maybe all of my subconscious speculation meant I really did want to see him—so I could be sure of how to dream the next time.

★

Over the next week I managed to avoid any contact with Johnny, even on the day he finally came to finish the painting. GG swore he did a good job, but I thought her glasses needed adjusting. In the bright light of day you could clearly see he missed a bunch of spots, left some serious streak marks here and there and careless splatters of new color where there wasn't supposed to be any at all. I was just relieved she hadn't noticed and demanded a do-over, which would mean he'd have to come back again. The last memory I had of him was how his tongue tasted like warm ashes and how he used his hipbone to keep me from moving away. Maybe I needed a new memory, a better one, yet I was afraid he'd end up saying something that would hurt me, and then I'd be forced to accept my role as the girl Johnny Lauten picked on.

I worked tonight. It was George's first day back. He looked a lot better than the last time we met, but I could still see the left-over bruises when he looked up toward the broken yellow ceiling tiles. We were on our break, sitting in the employee washroom area when I decided to tackle the subject one more time.

"So come on, George. Tell me what happened. Who was it that you had a fight with?"

He was playing with an unopened box of straws. "I told you—it doesn't matter. You don't know him anyway."

"How do you know?"

"I just do."

I leaned across the small lunch table and stared at him. "If you asked me a question, *any* question, I'd give you an honest answer."

"You would?" he asked.

"Yes."

"Okay then. Tell me, Chessie. Do you really have a boyfriend?"

For a minute I was honestly not sure. Johnny has kissed me twice in the past two weeks, and on the last day he was at our house I got the distinct impression he was peering through the windows trying to find me. Yet, if this was his definition of a girl-friend, it was unconventional at best and dismal at worst.

"Well, I guess, right now I'd have to say not really," I conceded. After all, you can't tell a lie when you're trying to prove a point about the truth.

"Can I ask you another question?"

"Go ahead."

He slipped his fingers in and out of the cardboard box top and took so long to speak again that I nearly forgot what we were talking about.

"George?"

"There's this formal dinner thing my family makes me go to every year. It's like a reunion, kind of. It's in two weeks on Sunday at four. Would you be willing to come with me, as a friend?"

You had to admire his tenacity. "I don't know, George. I really don't have anything formal to wear and I have no money to buy something new."

George looked up at me with his faded raccoon eye. I guessed I *could* wear my graduation dress. I sighed. "Maybe I might be able to go, *as a friend.*"

George smiled a little. Then he pulled his finger out of the box and spilled all the straws across the table and onto the floor.

He scrambled to reach for them. I picked up the ones that had fallen into my lap and handed them to him.

"Now it's my turn, George. And you *have* to answer. Who did that to you?"

Before he could reply, the buzzer rang announcing that our fifteen minutes was over. He jumped to his feet, but I reached over and grabbed his wrist. "*Who?*"

He shoved the last few straws into the box and then threw the entire thing into the trashcan. "Cole Harris," he said and turned to head into the restaurant.

Cole Harris? What reason could he possibly have to beat up on George?

"I do know him," I said, but George was already standing behind the counter.

✮

It was 11 p.m. and the house was still. I sat in the kitchen, in the dark, a band of baby buzz saws running through my head. It was the beginning of another episode. I didn't want to admit they were getting worse, not even to myself. I knew I had to go and see that doctor in St. Louis. GG kept bringing it up whenever we were alone. I think I was afraid of what he might tell me.

I thought about how George had asked me to that dinner thing. The only reason, the absolute one and only single reason I said yes was on account of those three little words—"as a friend." He was a nice guy, and we could end up being close, in a cousin-you-see-on-holidays way. Anything more would be a stretch. Not a leap, but a solid stretch at the very least. I thought it would be best if I didn't mention any of this to Meg yet. Even with my disclaimer firmly in place, I knew she'd freak out all the same. If a boy wasn't her type, then she'd be sure to insist he wasn't mine.

The buzzing was growing louder. I felt like my entire body was vibrating from the inside out. I almost hadn't realized Logan came into the room. The dark had swallowed me up, and I think for a minute I startled her, too.

"Oh hey, Chessie," she said.

"Hey, Logan." She was wearing pajamas she made out of an old Minnie Mouse T-shirt and a pair of gym shorts. Her hair shot up from the top of her head like a ponytail fountain.

"I got up for some water. How was work?"

"Pretty good, I guess."

She took a glass out of the cabinet and ran the tap. Listen Chessie, I wanted to talk to you about something."

"Sure. What's up?"

"I've been giving this whole matter with our father a lot of thought and I think I'd really like to see him."

"Are you sure?"

"Yup."

"Yeah. I think I'm going to see him too."

"I'm so glad we're going to do this together, Chessie. I have a feeling it'll be easier that way, don't you?"

"Yes. Easier."

She stared my way, lingering on my face. "Are you okay?"

The words were on my lips. No. I'm not. There's something terribly wrong.

"Just beat. Goodnight, Logan."

My bedroom was stifling and my body was on fire. I laid on the floor pretending it was a wooden box. I pretended ants and worms were crawling on me. I kept my mouth clamped shut. After a minute I jumped up, lunged for my notebook and pen, and wrote:

*4) I wish for a long and happy life.*

# Midnight Run

My room was too hot to sit in much less sleep. I flipped on the AC and went outside, onto the front porch to hail a cool breeze. The stuffy night air tossed a wandering mosquito my way but that was about it. The bad feeling had passed. For the moment I was the same old me. The girl with a plan—a plan going uncontrollably awry. I guessed I couldn't avoid St. Louis for much longer. And love, well, it seemed it was following its own course, a path undetermined by any wish I could write on a list or whisper from my heart.

The sound of a car engine broke my midnight trance.

I looked once and then twice. It was *him*; Johnny Lauten driving alone and slowing as he approached my house. His car crawled to a stop. His window was down and his forearm, tan and bulging veined, rested along the edge. He kept his voice low as he saw me there, on the steps of the porch he'd finished painting seven days ago.

"Chessie."

"Johnny."

"Whatcha doing?"

"I just got home from work. How about you?" My lips defaulted to nice at the mere sight of his.

"I'm cruising around…looking for…"

"For what?" I asked.

"Nothing in particular. Come here." I jumped to my feet.

I was keenly aware that I didn't have on a bra. As I got closer, I think he was keenly aware of it too. "You planning to turn in now?"

"No."

"You feel like taking a ride?"

I looked over my right shoulder at the house where my grandmother and sister were all tucked in.

"Or is it past your bedtime? Will Grandma be worried about you?" His smile dripped sugary sarcasm.I feared he was about to remind me that I was a baby again.

"I'll go," I said. "Give me a sec."

Without another thought I raced up the front steps and eased the front door closed. I dashed back to the passenger side of his pick up truck where he leaned over to unlock the door. Once inside, he shifted gears and we were off, charging down the street. Johnny had both hands on the wheel and a grin on his face.

Five minutes into our trip I nearly told him to turn around and take me home. It was quiet in the car, if you consider that his radio volume only went up to about medium-low. He kept his face forward. His mouth shut. *He's planning something. No, he's just being a careful driver.* My mind countered sense with nonsense. I guess you could say I heard what I needed to in order to keep me there. Eventually he spoke without moving his head. "I like the lake at this time of night."

"Is that where we're going? To the lake?" I asked.

"Yeah, but not this one. There's one a couple miles outside of Edenville. It's cool there."

"Cool?" At first I thought he was referring to the temperature, and I was glad since it was still like 100 degrees.

"Nobody's ever there. You can swim nude if you want to." His eyes sent me a slicing gleam. For the second time, I almost said I needed to go home. If he thought I would go skinny-dipping with him, he could think again. A half hour later we were sitting on the grass facing the water at a place I'd never seen before, and Johnny had his shirt off.

"You wanna smoke?"

"No, it's too late for that. If I do I'll get too tired," I said, thinking it was a pretty smooth excuse.

"Okay, then come on." He was on his feet and unbuttoning his jeans.

"Come on where?"

He continued to undress, slipping his pant legs off and then grasping the waistband of his underwear. "I'm going in," he said and in an instant he was as naked as the day he first met the world. I tried not to look at the area below where his belt had been.

"You coming in or what? The water's great," he called.

I was frozen. If I said no I'd be the baby he claimed I was. If I didn't, I was scared of where it might lead. Meg's voice boomed at me from inside my head. "I told you he just wants to have sex! He's a pig, I warned you!"

"Chessie? Are you scared?" He dropped his head below the surface before I could answer. I looked around hoping for a group of kids to pull up and rescue me, maybe a police car. But nobody showed. He was up again and pushing the wet hair off of his face. I searched for the moon. I was grateful it wasn't one of those full sloppy ones with the face in it that watches you. It was more like a smile hidden behind a bouquet of tree branches that blocked the light.

"What are you waiting for?"

"Nothing." I lifted my shirt over my head and tossed it onto the grass. My shorts were next. I left my panties on and ran to the water's edge, wading in as fast as I could. The lake slurped at my dry skin, licking me with its cool, wet tongue. I knew he was looking at me, and I couldn't look back. I got myself in, my bare chest covered up. He made his way over to me and put his hands on my shoulders. "Have you ever done this before?"

"Done what?"

"Swam naked with a guy."

My teeth wanted to chatter even though I wasn't cold. I refused to allow them to budge. I wanted to lie, though I didn't. "No, not really."

"You look real pretty here, with the water up around you."

He ran the tips of his fingers in a lazy figure eight along my collarbones, each time getting lower and closer to my breasts. In the distance a hoot owl called out to his hoot owl friends to come and see the show.

He let go of me then and took off cutting a path through the lake bed. I stood there unsure of what to do with myself aside from keeping my chin as close to the surface as I could. Water slipped in and out of my mouth, uninvited. Johnny circled around me like a hungry Great White sizing up a puny minnow. He went round and round until I spoke out.

"You're making me dizzy!"

He sprang up behind me and wrapped one arm around my waist.

"I like you, Chessie," he whispered into the crook of my neck. He ran his other hand up and across my chest. He pressed against me, against my backside and my panties that would probably never dry. I wasn't a prude. I'd been felt up before, but never underwater. He used skilled hands, hands of vast experience to touch me in a way that made me feel like mine were the first set of boobs he'd ever come in contact with.

I was keenly aware of his excitement, his twitching muscles, his uneven breath. He could have flipped me around, so we'd be face to face. And it would be unavoidable. We'd start to make out and we'd go further from there. In that very same instant his forearms directed me into a turn. My toes bent into the bottom of the lake, where the sharp, tiny rocks munched the bottom of my feet. I locked my knees, then my calves and my thighs. He slid his hands down, guiding me to where he hoped I'd go. When I didn't comply he changed his stance, in one fluid motion so he was before me. Not one sliver of cheesy moonlight could have fit between us. He drew me in, wrapping his legs around mine.

"Johnny," I began.

"Kiss me."

"Johnny, wait." A motor started somewhere out in the darkness. We weren't alone, even if it seemed that way.

"Come on, Chessie," he urged me in a voice that was thick and heavy. I made my mouth available, cautiously at first and then as if I were good at it. He reached for my underpants and tugged at the sides to roll them down.

"No Johnny…please, not here!"

I pulled away. He pulled me back.

"Why not here? Here is good."

I pulled away again. He pulled me in again.

"Listen. There are people out there."

"So what." His tone was higher then, and his grip less sweet.

"It's not right." I pushed at him and scratched his chest by accident, then apologized for it.

He backed up on his own and stared at me. His mouth was drawn to one side where his lip was cocked. "You gonna be a baby?"

"No, this isn't right. Not this way." One small tear welled up and I forced it back.

"Why not? Oh you *are* such a kid, Chessie! I thought you wanted to have a little fun. I should have brought your sister here instead. I bet she knows how to party."

With that I quickly moved out of the water and grabbed my shirt, holding it over my chest. "That's fine, Johnny. But she doesn't even like you at all." I stretched the top, like melted taffy, over my head. It clung to my wet skin.

He smiled and slowly emerged from the lake. "Really? That's not what she told me when I asked her out." He grabbed his collection of clothes off the ground taking a clump of loose green grass along with it and then beaming it toward the lake. As he dressed I looked away, slinked softly toward the truck, opened the door and slipped inside. He took forever to join me. He even smoked a cigarette first. Finally he was behind the wheel again. I kept my gaze steady at the floor where there was an assortment of half used matchbooks, three quarters, a pack of gum, a dollar bill and an empty water bottle.

"What's your deal? I thought you liked me."

I lifted my eyes up and over to him. "I do, Johnny. But you

don't care about me. You want to be here with somebody—anybody. And I just want to be here with *you*."

Two tears slipped out and raced each other down my face. My legs were shaking. He placed his hand on top of my thigh.

"That's sweet. You're sweet. Come here." He gathered me in to his chest and held me there for a minute. Then he let go. "I'll take you home now."

I nodded, and he sent me back to my original position. He didn't say another thing until he put the car in neutral and idled outside of my front door.

"Okay, well…see ya."

I waited to hear more yet there wasn't any. "Yeah…see ya," I replied and darted for the porch as he hustled away. I prayed he was quiet, but I heard the screech as he sliced the bend in the road. I remembered how late it was and that I was half dressed and completely soaked. If GG were to hear me I'd probably be in tons of trouble.

I reached up to get the extra key we kept hidden over the post closest to the doorjamb. I felt around here and there. My heartbeat skipped. It was gone.

Our emergency hide-a-key was missing in action. I dropped to my knees and searched the floor. I had no idea how I would get in and I couldn't very well knock or ring the bell. I tiptoed around back to try the kitchen door. In all the years I'd lived here GG had never once forgotten to lock it, yet I held out some teeny strand of hope that this would be the one night it had slipped her mind. Naturally, there was no such luck.

I wanted to panic. More than that, I wanted to cry. I imagined what I would have to say to GG in the morning when she found me there huddled on the porch floorboards. I was sleepwalking and got locked out? I thought I heard a prowler and came outside to check and the door locked behind me? A prowler in Eden's Pond? It was clear to me that I'd made a huge mistake sneaking off with Johnny in the strange, heated pre-dawn hours. Yet, as I stood there, shivering, saturated and exhausted, it occurred

to me that during the entire time I was with him I hadn't given
the Big S a single thought, not a one. I was just a girl. Not a sick
girl. Just a girl.

I had no idea if he was in love with me. Chances are he was
using me. Truth was, I had such little experience either way it
was almost impossible for me to know the difference.

I knew only one thing for sure. I sure liked the way it felt with
his body pressed up against mine.

## Curly Fries

GG's prized peony bush clung to the light pink aluminum siding on the back of the house. She'd planted it along with a dainty white birch in honor of my mother, six years ago. It was so big now, apparently growing strong. She'd kill me if I smashed it by climbing through the window to Logan's room. Still, it was obvious that if I didn't, I'd be spending the rest of the night locked outside. I reached my fist up as far as I could, arching my back so I wouldn't lean into the delicate greenery. I tapped softly against the pane calling her name in my quietest voice. "Logan...Logan it's me, it's Chessie. Logan, are you awake?"

When I got no response I repeated my request, this time at a different octave. After a moment or two, the lamp light flickered and I heard her coming toward me.

"Chessie?" she asked through the glass.

"Yes! Yes, it's me. I got locked out. Help me."

She opened the window, which jerked and heaved, and then the screen, which squealed at me. "What happened? Are you okay?"

"Shhh... Yes, I don't want to wake GG. Can you help me?"

"I think so."

I stepped onto a cinder block that was propped under the gutter spout, giving myself a leg up. Logan grabbed my arms the rest of the way. I was inside within minutes and I helped her close the window once again.

"Is it raining?" she asked, checking me over with a puzzled look in her eyes.

"No, I uh. I, all right—listen, if I tell you where I went, you have to promise not to say a word to my grandmother, or anyone for that matter."

She sat on the edge of her bed, and I sat in GG's sewing chair with the pincushion armrests still in the corner of the room. "I promise," she said.

"I went to this lake…with Johnny. We went for a swim."

"And…"

"And that's it. I mean he was trying to get me to have sex with him. He tried really, really hard."

Logan's bottom jaw dropped open. "Did you even have your bathing suit with you?"

"No, I wasn't really expecting to go. He came along while I was out on the front steps earlier tonight, after work."

"So then you went in…" she began.

"We went in without our clothes on," I admitted. I don't know why. I needed to say it out loud to someone and it couldn't be Meg.

She nodded, her eyes growing wider. "I never did that before."

I stood up and checked myself out in the small mirror nailed to the backside of her door. "Neither have I." I still looked like the old me, the one that wouldn't be caught dead in the water without the proper attire. But there I was, a new version of the old me with my hair all tousled and stringy and damp, my T-shirt stuck to my breasts in two round wet spots, my nipples standing at attention and my shorts wearing the outline of my panties that had lived to tell.

"You should go and change in case Ghita gets up," she suggested.

"Yeah, I'm pretty beat. I'm going to bed." I looked behind me and then behind her, at the table she used to hold her things. A small silver frame was hugging a photo of a beautiful woman with smooth caramel colored skin and big green eyes.

I knew in an instant it was Logan's mother since Logan looked just like her.

"That's her. That's my mom. She was going to school there, in

Spain," Logan began, "to the Complutense University of Madrid. She was studying journalism. She dreamed of becoming a famous reporter. That's how she met him. Eventually she had to quit. It was too hard to be a student and a single mother of a small child at the same time."

"She's gorgeous," I said. Logan nodded. "How did she die?"

"Breast cancer. By the time they found it, it was too late to save her."

"I'm sorry…about your mom."

"Me, too. I'm sorry for both of us."

I wanted to wrap her up in my arms, where the fine hairs stuck up like a freshly mowed lawn. Yet it felt too presumptuous so I stepped away. "Goodnight, and thanks Logan."

She nodded again. "Goodnight, Chess."

Once upstairs, I stripped the wet clothes from my body and grabbed the picture of me and my mother—the one Logan gave me shortly after she arrived. There beneath my mother's casual smile was the very same look Logan's mom had. I figured it was the residue of Mark Madrid and his way of breaking dreams and hearts all at once. I wondered if Johnny Lauten would grow into a man who left his mark on women scattered in random places, and if Mark Madrid ever took my mother on a moonlit swim without her clothes.

✵

Logan and GG were up at nine for services at ten a.m. It felt ungodly to me, as I stumbled down the stairs, to have to be any place at ten in the morning. Yet the two were awake, alive and chatty as they prepared to leave. GG surveyed me and straightened her own back as though it would help me with my posture as I slumped into a kitchen chair.

"Are you all right, Chessie?" she asked, peering over the edge of her glasses.

"Fine."

"I don't suppose you'd like to come along with us to services today?"

"You mean the services that are in thirty minutes?" I should have stayed in bed and slept in but I had to pee and the only bathroom was on the first floor.

"Yes."

Logan watched me, offering a knowing glance. It said, "I remember last night, and I won't say a word."

"I don't think so."

GG clucked her tongue against her teeth. "That's too bad. I was hoping to take you and Logan out for a bite afterward."

I hadn't even realized she went a little light on the usual breakfast buffet. In fact, aside from the orange juice and coffee, there was only a bowl of apple cinnamon oatmeal on the counter.

"Why?" I asked.

"For a treat. We could go and have some pot pies at Gloria's on Main Street."

GG loved to eat at Gloria's Place. It was Eden's Pond's answer to a diner except with home style cooking. Gloria is Mrs. Delafield's sister-in-law in that she was married to dead Mr. Delafield's brother. I mostly just ate their ham steaks and curly fries. The pot pies tasted like a baked shoe dumped in a shell.

"You girls can get a huge plate of curly fries," she added, doing that mind reading thing again.

It seemed like there was something bigger than pot pies and fries going on, so I decided to say yes.

"Oh good. Now hurry and get dressed. We don't want to be stuck in the last pew. You can hardly hear anything back there." She disappeared down the hall and into her bedroom, and Logan grabbed my arm.

"I guess we could tell her at lunch," she was speaking in a hushed tone, using her church voice already.

"Tell her what?"

"About how we want to see Mark."

I had nearly forgotten that conversation, the one Logan and I had where we agreed to give him an audience. Was that still the plan? It seemed so much had changed overnight. I had seen a whole new side of Johnny—actually I had seen every side of Johnny and he had seen nearly all of me. I had visions of his dimensions, perfectly proportioned and eager.

"Oh, okay sure, whatever." I scurried up the stairs to get dressed.

As I changed out of my pajama shirt, I stood before my vanity, topless, having a look at myself. He'd been there, touching me. I could not erase the memory of how he looked as he strutted out of the lake, and I could not help wanting to see more of him. For the first time in my life, my PG-rated head was filled with X-rated thoughts, all of which starred Johnny and me. If I hadn't stopped him, most of these or at the very least ONE of these things may have actually happened. And then what? Would Johnny have fallen in love with me? When I told him I had to leave, would he beg me not to go?

"Chessie! We're going to be late!" GG bellowed.

I pulled on a pair of my most respectable cotton cropped pants. Perhaps spending some time in God's house that morning would do my dirty mind good.

✶

It turned out that the antidote to raging teenage hormones was lunch with your grandmother or curly fries or both. As we sat on the sticky brown leather bench seats in our favorite booth at Gloria's, Logan and I together on one side and GG across the table, I regained my composure bite by bite. Logan was building up to her big announcement when, midway through her chicken shoe pie, GG with the fork still up at the side of her mouth, made one of her own. "I heard from your father last night. He's here."

I turned my head and swept the room with my eyes.

"No, not here in this restaurant, not even here in Eden's Pond. Here in Missouri. It seems he has other business to take care of, so he made the trip out."

I kept my words pitched down. "Why? Are there some other kids here he's trying to claim?"

Logan shifted around as if she wanted to get up and run.

GG just continued. "He said there's no pressure however if you girls have made any decisions…"

"We have. We decided we'll see him." Logan spoke out so loudly I think she surprised herself.

My grandmother fixed her gaze at me and I stared back until I needed to look away. She knew that of all the people in my life, there was only one I held responsible for almost every bad thing there was in the world, in *my* world, and that was Mark Madrid. If it were possible I'd swear he was the reason I got the Big S, although medically speaking I didn't think so.

"Are you sure, Chessie?" she asked with her baby's breath tone.

"Yup," I answered and proceeded to jam two fries in my mouth simultaneously.

That was so I wouldn't say anything more. I wouldn't say that I'd been waiting for what felt like a million years to see for myself what Mark Madrid was made of. I practiced patience and rehearsed my verbal assault until I had it down to a science. I'd know where to pause, when to look at him and when not to. I'd even anticipated his reply. "I'm sorry, Chessie. I wish I had made better choices."

Logan coughed then drank her water.

"Well all right, I suppose I'll see when he can come." GG looked either pained or pleased, I couldn't decide which. When Gloria appeared at the end of our table to meet Logan, I was certain she was pleased again.

"This is our young Logan," GG said, taking credit for the child of the son-in-law who cheated on her daughter. It was bizarre indeed, although you had to excuse a woman with a heart so big she could look past the odd circumstances and find her pride.

✯

After lunch, we went home and Logan sped off for a run. GG followed me around for fifteen minutes like a hungry pup after a fresh bone until I stopped short at the bottom of the stairs.

She was doing the St. Louis hop.

"When do you want to go?" I asked her.

"How is this Tuesday? We could do it in one day. It's only two hours each way. I could be the co-pilot."

"Fine, fine." I gathered my hair, lifted it off my neck and tied it into a ponytail with a band I had around my wrist.

"And Chessie, what if we tell Logan?"

"No. No way."

GG had a snag in her pantyhose that spanned the entire length of her leg. Her eyes looked smaller or sunk deeper into her skull. "But she's family. We could take her with us. Maybe she could do the driving."

"I'm capable of doing it. I'm not dead yet!" The words were out before I could pull them back. The very punch of them set her off balance and she grabbed hold of the banister to steady herself. "I'm sorry," I added.

"Chessie. You're not going to die. You are *not* going to die!" The panic in her voice sent a sharp pang through my chest. And just when she repeated it for the third time, Logan returned in time to hear her.

GG excused herself and retreated to her room. Logan's face was one huge inquisition as she looked past me to GG and then me again. "Chess, is everything alright?"

## Question Eight

I could have told Logan right then. Maybe I should have. But she smelled ripe with fresh summer air and her cheeks had a bright pink stripe down the middle. The energy inside of her was highly visible. She was a rechargeable battery, one of those you plug in when it's running low and it powers up again without a hitch. Me? I was a cheap package of triple A's from the dollar store, the kind that expires after you use them for a week. I was angry at the disparity, angry at GG for wanting to break our code of silence.

"Nothing. Everything is fine," I answered and climbed the stairs without another word.

✭

We left at 7 a.m. on Tuesday morning for St. Louis under a sky full of immaculate sunshine. I assigned the handling of excuses to GG, who said she told Logan we had financial business to tend to and that we'd be home by suppertime. Logan offered to have dinner ready for us when we got back, some Louisiana dish she knew how to prepare.

I'd never been there before, to that part of Missouri. The only thing I even cared at all to see was the airport. If the Big S was also a Big Liar, then I was going to learn to fly planes so that one day, when I was older, I could have wings of my own. Though for now I had to keep my feet on the tarmac. St. Louis was like a big city with lots of big city people in a hurry to get someplace important. I suppose we had somewhere important to go, too.

His name was Dr. Pigeon, which initially I thought was hysterical and then realized wasn't all that funny. He was younger than Doc Abner, maybe 40 at best, and his hair wasn't purchased at the beauty supply. It was fully attached to his head, dark blond with teeth comb marks running through it. He took my vitals and a sample of nearly every fluid I had in my body. There were two nurses at his beck and call, fluttering around me with obedient, busy smiles. Doc Abner didn't even have one nurse, only his wife who doubled as a receptionist/appointment maker.

Doctor Pigeon studied the notes Dr. Abner had forwarded. He read them over and over while GG and I sat quietly, GG clutching her purse in her lap, her legs crossed at the ankle. She was Jello-Mold Grandma, all coagulated and stiff. After a solid eight minutes he looked up.

"I think an aggressive path of treatment is in order here."

"How aggressive, Doctor?" GG asked.

"I would alter her meds, monitor her x-rays and watch her very closely." He spoke as if I wasn't in the room, which made me feel invisible.

GG fingered the tissue attached to her watchband. "Is this a course of action Doctor Abner can perform?"

"I'll need to conference with him at his earliest convenience. We can advise you after that. Do you have any questions, Chessie?"

I had a quick glance at my grandmother who was doing her best to keep from melting all over his white tile floor. "Can I beat this?"

Doctor Pigeon removed his tortoise-rimmed glasses and laid them on his desk. "You've done remarkably well under the circumstances."

"Thank you, but that's a statement, not an answer, Doctor. Can I beat this? Is there any shot at all?"

He hesitated, looked from GG and back to me. "A long one."

On the drive home I put on GG's favorite radio station, the one that played only old Frank Sinatra songs. She knew all the words although I guess she wasn't in the mood to sing along.

Logan had the table set and ready for us, and a saucepan full of pork, rice and beans on the stove top.

"Was it a good day?" she asked to either one of us.

GG and I replied at once. "A long one."

✫

It was turning into the week from hell. First I had to meet Dr. Pigeon, which in and of itself wasn't awful except that for the first time in months I felt only half-alive.

Then Meg, who went to the Krazy Kutz in Edenville and had her hair cut and died bright blue, told me Johnny and Sara were back together again, which led me to believe that Wish Number Two wasn't panning out all that well. She elaborated on how her big brother, the Perv, took his on-again/off-again girl downstairs and they kicked up so much noise that Meg had to leave the house. The last thing I wanted to think about was Johnny and Sara and how he had sex with her in his bedroom with the cardboard over the window. Yet my mind would not comply. The memory of his hands around my waist and across my chest made me feel cheap and excited all at the same time. He was a serial cheater, no doubt, and speaking of which, the cheater to top them all was about to pay a visit. Mark Madrid was coming to the house on Thursday night at 6 p.m. It was the week from hell if there ever was one.

I tossed into my sheets, winding them around my body on Wednesday night when I was supposed to be sleeping. The air conditioner grumbled against the sides of the window frame. I meant to shove a sock in there earlier to keep it quiet but forgot to. I felt the early signs of another episode churning in my chest and I laid on my belly to see if I could make it stop. The last time I checked it was 2 a.m.

"Chessie?"

My mother's voice. I spun around, aware that I was in a dream and yet fully awake. "Mama, where have you been? I've been waiting to see you again."

"I'm right there with you all the time." I couldn't see her as well as I had before. This time she looked as if she were painted in the air, all pastel brushstrokes and warm shadows. "All the time?" I asked, thinking maybe she knew about what I did with Johnny at the lake.

"Yes, my darling, all the time."

"Logan is here and Mark is coming. I don't know what to do, Mama. Maybe I wished wrong."

"No. You're doing everything right. Don't worry."

"What's going to happen to me? Can't you say? Please tell me."

"Keep the faith, Chessie, keep your heart's desire close and always know I won't ever leave you."

"But you *did* leave me. I don't want you to be there, wherever you are now. I want you here with me and GG." I was crying fat salty tears like when I was little and I skinned my knee. "I miss you so much but I don't want to die!"

"Chessie, I love you. There's nothing to fear." I felt her arms around me in that instant and though I tried to hug her too I wasn't able. If so I wouldn't let go. I'd make her stay with me through it all for whatever fate had in store.

"I love you too, Mama."

It lasted less than a minute. I'd waited so long to speak to her and she left all too soon.

Still, for some odd reason I felt at peace. There was something in the sound of her words, something smooth and delicate, like an answer to a prayer.

✸

Logan made a list with a heading she'd underlined in bold black ink.

It said, "Things to ask my father" and she wasn't the least bit embarrassed by her organization. She had it on the table all morning, adding to it until, the last I saw, she was at number 10. She let me look it over and kept chattering all the while.

"Is it all right? Am I being too rough? Too easy? Feel free to add your own questions, Chessie."

"They're fine. They're all fine." The truth was I had no questions and there were no answers. On the morning of the day of the coming of Mark Madrid I had only one goal—don't throw up. If I could keep my food down all the while he was here then I'd consider the meeting a success.

GG served an early supper so we'd be cleaned up by six. It was during our meal she revealed she wasn't planning to stay home for the big night.

"What? Why not?" I asked.

"I think it's best you girls have some privacy. I'll be at Mrs. Delafield's if you need me."

So my grandmother had chosen to strategically remove herself from the festivities. I was mad that she wasn't planning to stand behind me or beside me for moral support.

"I think you should be here," I said, tiny razor blades attached to my words.

"This night is about you the two of you and your father. If I'm here it'll evolve into something more."

I had forgotten that my grandmother had her own list of issues with Mark and it had possibly a hundred items on it.

By the time 5:45 rolled around GG was long gone, leaving us with a reminder of how she would be "only a telephone call away."

I wondered if there was a right outfit to wear when one met their father for the first time in fifteen years. Without thinking I had put on jean shorts and a red polo shirt, and I thought that was fine until I saw Logan waiting in the living room in a plaid skirt and white cotton blouse. She looked like she was ready to go to Sunday school or something. I wasn't sure if she remembered the same Mark Madrid that I did, the guy who thought dressing up meant wearing coveralls without holes in the knees. I didn't have the heart to remind her, since she seemed so distracted with her list resting in her lap and her eyes darting toward the door every time a car passed by.

At 6:05 Logan got up and began to pace the floor. At 6:10 she fiddled with the lining of her skirt and at 6:15 she proclaimed, "He isn't coming," and went into her bedroom long enough to come back out in black silk running shorts and a silver nylon top.

"It was a good list Logan, a really good list," I told her. And just as I started to climb the steps to my room, a car door slammed. I stopped in my path. Logan stood up, then sat down, then stood up again. Finally, at 6:25 p.m. Mark Madrid knocked at our front door. I began to head for it, yet my feet wouldn't move. "I can't," I whispered.

Logan swallowed and got up off the chair. Her shorts made shushing sounds as she walked. She opened the door slowly as though she thought something might jump out at her.

He wasn't wearing coveralls or a ponytail or even a smile. Mark Madrid looked about as serious as a man sentenced to the electric chair and taking his last spin around the block.

"Hello," he said.

"Hello," she replied and stepped aside for him to enter.

He wasn't as tall as my memory served, but he was still more legs than body. He was thin except for a small pouch of extra gut he wore in his midsection. His hair was shorter now, just below his ears, and slicked back with some sort of wet stuff that looked crunchy. There was a patch of brownish grey stubble over his chin. I thought of GG, who always said she never trusted a man with hair on his face since he probably had something to hide.

He stepped toward the room and then stopped as if he were awaiting direction. I found my legs and then my feet and then my words in that order. "You can come in and sit down."

He looked me over, his eyes falling at the corners. "Thank you, Francesca." He took a seat on the sofa. I made my way over to Logan. We stood side by side.

"It's amazing to see the two of you at once, together," he said.

I wondered how long it took him to pick out the brown and beige checkered shirt he was wearing and the dark blue jeans. Did he change more than once or simply go with the first thing he chose? "Logan, you're so tall now. I always knew you would be. And Chessie…you're a picture of your mother."

It was Logan who eventually broke the breathless silence that saturated the air. "I had so many things, so many questions to ask you…but I don't know how to do this now."

"I was hoping to spend some time alone with each one of you, individually. Maybe you would both be more comfortable that way," he said.

I looked at Logan who had the paper crumpled in between her fingers. She was rolling down the top edge over and over until it had a permanent curl. "I'll go walking for a little while," I told her.

"Are you sure, Chess?" she asked gently.

I nodded and gave her a touch on the arm. He was smiling at us, and for a minute it made me angry. "What is it? Why are you smiling like that?" I asked.

He shook his head. "I don't know. I wasn't sure what to expect of you girls, although you seem to be getting along just fine."

"Why wouldn't we?" I moved toward the door.

"Well…I suppose I made an assumption," he replied, without the defensiveness I imagined.

"Are there any more of us? Are there any more children that you have or don't have or had once and left with somebody else to raise?" Logan had jumped from question number one to number eight without a hitch. I didn't see it coming, particularly the way she delivered it with all the power her sturdy body could muster.

I turned to see the look on his face. She'd asked the one thing I wanted to hear him answer.

"Well, yes and no, Logan. Yes, I have another child—a son—his name is Max, although I haven't left him for his mother to raise. He's eleven months old and he lives with me and my wife, Anne."

The punch landed somewhere around my lower left side and I wondered if his reply had punctured a kidney or something. Suddenly, at 6:40 p.m. on Thursday night there were Anne and Max—two more players in an already dysfunctional game—and I was seething. I had to leave, immediately. And I knew just where I was heading.

I gave one last check on Logan who had dropped her list on the floor.

"I'll be back," I told her just before I fled for Mrs. Delafield's.

# The Bee Won't Sting

I ran down the streets of Eden's Pond, pounding the roadway so hard the heels of my feet were burning by the time I reached Mrs. Delafield's walkway. I assumed that since GG missed her usual teatime on account of our early supper, I'd find her out in the yard, past the rose arbor. Walking slowly felt odd to me as I made my way gingerly toward the sound; two ladies chirping like a couple of happy birds perched on a straw nest. I wondered if I needed to knock to signal my arrival, in case they were discussing private stuff. It turned out I heard Mrs. Delafield complaining about her knee pain and how the cost of milk is going up.

"Hello?" I called out and in an instant the chirping came to an abrupt stop.

"Chessie?" GG called.

My pace quickened as I neared them. They weren't nestled on a bed of twigs but lounging on two wrought iron chairs, guarding their steaming cups of tea. The sun was still hanging there in the middle of the sky, and my grandmother had her back to it. In that light she seemed translucent, sheer like the nylon drapes she'd hung in the dining room we only used on special occasions.

"What is it? Are you all right?"

Mrs. Delafield had gained weight since I saw her last, and she looked out at me over her two deflated basketball breasts and smiled. "My goodness, Chessie! Aren't you a sight for old lady eyes! How's that Shadow treating you? My Henry never could get her up over 45."

"The car is fine, thanks. I'm sorry to barge in… GG can I talk to you for a minute…alone?"

"Of course." GG struggled to her feet, using the table to push herself up.

"No, no you both sit right here. I have to go inside and check on my strudel." Mrs. Delafield stepped aside and offered me her chair. I took it, although I didn't want to. I knew that even from her kitchen she'd be desperate to overhear. With that in mind I forced myself to whisper.

"Did you know about his wife and baby? Did you know about them?"

GG blinked once, took a breath and a very long minute to get seated again. "Yes, I did. I just found out. I wanted to tell you, however he asked if he could be the one to do that."

"So you're keeping secrets with *him* now, is that it? I don't understand. I thought you hated Mark Madrid. I thought you blamed him for taking Mom away."

"I'm admittedly not a fan of your father's, I won't dispute that. Still I believe there's room in life for more than one chance at things."

"That's what she said; that's what my mother told me before she left to see him and look where it got her…"

"Please, calm down. So your father has a family now, *for* now. Think about it. His child isn't even a year old yet. He was with you until you were three-and-a-half and with Logan for less time than that. What makes you think he can hold onto a family of his own *suddenly* when he's never been able to before?"

The grating on the chair was digging into my skin. I sat up and wriggled my thighs. Strudel called to me from the kitchen window. I despised strudel. "I don't know. Maybe he's changed."

GG took the tissue out from under her watchband and dabbed at the sides of her forehead and mouth. "Things change. People don't change. They shift, like the sand in an egg timer. The timer tips, they move to accommodate. But inside they're still made of the same grain."

"GG…"

She batted her eyelids at me as if she was preparing to be struck.

"GG, does Mark know about me being sick? Please be honest. Did you tell him?"

My grandmother was as perfectly still as I'd ever seen her; like a statue made of a billion tiny grains of 65 year-old sand. "Chessie, please understand. I did what I felt was the best thing. He's your father—"

"NO! No he isn't. He's nothing to me. You had no right!" I was on my feet, breathing hard, thinking that I might scream or burst in two. "Who else did you tell?" I looked behind me toward the house. "Does Mrs. Delafield know too?"

"No, no, of course not."

"I trusted you. I never thought you'd do this to me." A giant wad of anger had welled up in the back of my throat. I swallowed it down only to find it still there a second later.

"Chessie, please—"

Before either of us could say another word, Mrs. Delafield appeared in the doorframe.

"Oh Chessie? Are you going so soon?"

I closed my eyes, just long enough to be pretend-well again. "Yes. It was good to see you again."

"You too. Don't be such a stranger."

I felt GG's eyes on me until I disappeared from her sight. All along, deep down inside, my gut had been badgering me about what I wanted to believe versus what I feared believing. I wanted to think that GG and I had an iron-clad agreement, that she'd keep our secret, take it to my grave. I was too scared to think anything else. What did it mean if GG could lie to me? It made everything in my world slanted. All truths were uneven, off center and deranged. I ran down the corner and crumbled onto the pavement, my head buried between my elbows. I knew what was waiting for me. I knew *who* was waiting. It didn't matter whether he knew or not. I would fulfill Wish Number Three either way.

✦

Mark was sitting on the front porch. I turned onto my street and there he was. Mark Madrid, recently acquired father of three. I didn't notice Logan and I wondered if he had sent her off and running too. He watched me approach and stood up as I arrived.

"Are you okay, Francesca?"

"I'm fine. Where's Logan?"

"In the house. I thought we could take a walk, if you like."

"We don't have to. We can sit right here." I moved past him and over to the rocker. I was making him pop up and down like a puppet. It felt good to control him.

"The old place hasn't changed much," he said looking around.

"We had the porch painted."

"I meant the town, the streets, the village. It's so familiar."

"It's pretty simple here. I guess Last Chance is more interesting huh?"

"Not terribly. Besides, I was only there temporarily."

"There's a shock." I intended to say this beneath my breath but it rang out clear as day.

He took his hit and rallied enough to reply. "Chessie, I know you're angry with me. I can't say I blame you. Every child deserves a full set of parents. I know I failed you. What can I say? There aren't the right words to begin to explain or make due."

"I would think by now you would have found the right words. I would think with all the places you've been and people you've acquired, you would have gathered up a whole slew of right words." I refused to look into his face. I kept my gaze just over his left shoulder. I saw where Johnny slapped his brush on the rotting wood post.

"I have learned some things about myself over the years. I've learned that not every man is meant to fly planes."

"So you're a pilot now?"

"No. I'm using that as a metaphor."

"So by flying planes you mean not every man is meant to be a father."

He nodded. I thought he'd nearly given up trying to catch my eye.

"Well, it's awfully inconvenient to realize this after you've already left the ground."

"I agree."

"And now you've done it again. Max is it? Does Max know that his daddy can't fly?"

For a second, he squirmed. I wasn't planning to turn up the heat so soon but he kept looking at me with a pity in his eyes that came from knowing something he shouldn't.

"Max is a great baby with a great mother."

"So surely *she* can take over at any time? Surely she can fly solo right?"

"I know I deserve this, I do. Still, can't you at least try to be civil? I understand it's been hard on you, without your mother for so long and…"

My body couldn't hold steady any longer. I rose to my feet again, "Don't even say it. Don't go there. You don't have the right to care about me or my life. And my mother, you didn't care about her either. She was going to see you because she thought you could love her again. She thought you wanted us back. So she went out and bought a pretty new dress. It was yellow with tiny white flowers on it. She was so worried that you would like it and that she looked perfect for you. She wore it that day even though she was afraid it might wrinkle. She wanted it to be the first thing you saw her in!"

"Chessie, I'm sorry…"

"You never came. After the accident, you never even came!"

"I wanted to, but Ghita wouldn't have it. She told me to stay away. She said it was all my fault. I told her I wanted to come and be with you. It was your grandmother that said no."

"I don't need you now either!" This time I looked straight

at him. I didn't want to see my own eyes there, in his. But I saw mine, and Logan's too. He bowed his head and stared down at his feet. "I don't want you to need me, Francesca. Though I'd like you to accept me."

I didn't answer and he went on. "I was a lousy father, I know that. And I'm not sure if I'll do Max any good. However I did love your mother, in my way; I love all of my children, in my way. I'd like you to accept me for who I am…without hating me for who I'm not."

There was a buzzing in the air around me, and I saw the responsible bee milling over my head. I willed it to sting me—anyplace—just one sting would do.

But you can't wish for a sting anymore than you can wish for somebody to love you, or perhaps anymore than a wish can spare your life.

"Do you think you can find it in your heart to accept me?"

I turned away from him, edging for what was left of the porch, trying to put more space between us. I looped my arm around the rail, hugging it as if there were some chance it would hug me back and inviting splinters that didn't come either.

"My heart won't have a thing to do with you. If I accept you, it'll be because I allow my mind to, only my mind."

"Well, that's a start." I heard his footsteps behind me. I shrank into the rail so he'd move away, yet when I looked around he was only inches from my body.

"I want you and Logan to be able to reach me if you have to."

"Why would we have to do that?"

"I don't know. Just in case."

"GG has your number."

"Okay. I guess I'll be taking off then. Thanks for the talk, Chessie. It was really wonderful to see you again."

He lifted his arms, and in spite of my glare, hung them around me.

"Don't," I told him.

"I'm sorry." He started down the stairs and over to his car, and then turned around. "I really am so sorry. For everything."

He left me with one of those dopey, pathetic frowns, the kind I'd been hoping to avoid. It was only me and the bee on the porch and then suddenly even the bee had flown away. I should have been sad or mad for what the evening had brought. Yet something inside of me was happy. I'd lashed out at him, gave him a good "what for," as GG liked to say. And maybe the fact that he knew I was sick would make his suffering that much deeper.

## Pigeons & Polar Bears

Meg has said that her mother is the most gullible person in the world. Yet Mrs. Lauten didn't buy that it was the mono making Meg's hair turn blue even though that's what Meg told her. They wound up having a terrible fight since Mrs. Lauten tried to enforce a punishment Meg argued she's too old for.

"This is the exact reason I should be going away to school in September. I really have to escape the tyranny, Chess." We compared stories, up in my bedroom, on Sunday night after we got over giggling at how GG reacted to Meg's new look.

"Is that a wig you have on your head?" she asked.

"No, Mrs. Barraco, it's my actual hair."

"Is that how the kids are wearing it these days? Call me old fashioned, but I liked it the other way. This looks like you fell over into a vat of wild blueberry Kool-Aid."

Meg was lying on my bed, tummy side up, toes pointed up at the ceiling. "You should really look into going to that aviary school, Chess."

"It's aviation school."

"What did I say?"

"You said aviary. That's like a giant bird cage."

"Whatever…you should go. And you know what else? I'm glad you told your father off. I still can't believe he got another woman to marry him. So that makes three wives, right?"

"Two. He never married Logan's mother."

"Wow…then she's a bastard child!"

"SHHH!" I heaved a pillow at her.

"In any case, she's a bitch."

"No. She isn't either."

"Okay, a bitchlet." That was Meg's word for when some girl was just a little bit bitchy.

"No."

"You're being a bitchlet." She flung the pillow back at me.

Five minutes later there was a knock at my door.

"Let me," Meg said and rushed to open it. "Oh hey, Logan."

"Hi Meg…Chessie, I wanted to tell you that I'm going into town with Ghita for a while."

"Okay, sure," I said.

"Why don't you hang here with us, Logan? We're going to paint our nails to match my hair."

"I already told Ghita I'd go with her. Thanks anyway."

Meg grabbed Logan by the wrist and pulled her into the bedroom. "Oh come on, Logan. Really, you must be dying to have some fun. I'll bet you're starting to miss your friends in Louisiana by now."

I snuck up behind Meg and pinched her on the arm. "Logan, you can stay with us if you like. You don't have to polish your nails or anything."

"That's all right, Chessie, and yes, Meg, I am missing my friends from home, but not for long. My best friend, Allie, is due back from Australia in about four weeks and then I'll be moving there to stay with her."

"You are?" Meg asked.

I looked at her—my half sister—and checked her face to see if I thought she was making it up. I didn't. "You are?" I asked.

"Yeah. I'll see you guys later," she said and walked away. Just like that I was informed that my brand new sister was leaving me.

★

I didn't work with George again until Monday, the five p.m. shift, which meant we would have to close. He had a car with him this time, so I wouldn't get stuck driving him home. I had completely forgotten about the Sunday dinner thing coming up at the end of the week. But he hadn't. We were behind the counter when he brought it up.

"So I can pick you up at your house if you want," he said. He was counting the money in the register even though it wasn't time to do that yet.

"What? Pick me up when?"

"On Sunday, for the dinner dance."

"Oh…is that this Sunday?"

"Yes." He smiled a little.

"It's a dance too?" I ran a warm rag over the dots of dried ketchup stuck to the faux wood countertop.

"Well they have a local band that plays and some people dance."

"I don't," I said quickly.

"Um yeah, me neither," he said, though I thought he was lying.

"Couldn't I just meet you there?"

"I guess…it's really no trouble for me to come and get you."

"George. I'll take my own car, okay?"

"Okay." I watched him stay busy enough so he didn't have to look at me. Having him pick me up would be way too much like a date. It was over the top. We were friends. *Friends.*

"What happened between you and Cole Harris?" I needed to change the subject since George was about to disappear into himself.

"It was nothing."

"It was something enough."

"Look Chessie, it's behind me now. None of the details matter." For the first time since I met him I heard George sound annoyed. With me.

"Okay fine, George. Suit yourself. I was trying to be decent, all right?"

My minor retaliation had unnerved him. George rushed at me from the ice cream machine and began to spill it like he'd been shot with truth serum. "He came in here one night when I was working and you weren't. He was acting like a moron, talking lots of crap. I told him to shut his mouth, and he left. Then he came back later on, when I was leaving and took me off guard in the parking lot after everyone was gone.

"He's such a jerk. He's not normal you know."

"I know."

"Well, I hope you got a few punches in too."

"I did—I did," he insisted, although I was sure he was lying again. He took a pen and paper from under the counter, scrawled some words across the page and handed it to me. "This is the name and address of the place the dinner will be. It starts at four. And that's my phone number, in case you have any trouble finding it or if you change your mind about a ride."

I stuck the paper down deep in my pocket. "K, thanks."

I tried to imagine what I'd do if George wanted to kiss me. Then I wondered why I was even imagining a thing like that.

✴

On Tuesday morning GG cooked every morsel of food in our kitchen and set it out for just us three. Logan and I shared a question mark in our eyes and as much scrambled eggs, toast, home fries, bacon and sausage we could stuff into our mouths. GG took one bite of a grapefruit, cleared her place and then her throat.

"Mrs. Delafield is having her knee operation tomorrow. She asked if I could stay with her for a few days to help her out. Will you girls be okay here without me?"

"We'll be fine," Logan said.

Since the day I'd confronted her in the garden at Mrs. D's things between GG and I had been strained. It was the first time ever in my life I'd been so upset with her. We were existing in a brand new universe where my grandmother was somebody I almost didn't know. Our conversations were watered down and only if mandatory. She wanted to apologize and I wanted to forgive her. Yet it was too much, too little, too late, too hard. Her food was a place to put the words neither of us could manage.

"Yeah, we will," I offered, more for Logan's sake.

GG still had no idea Logan was planning to go home soon. She would take it personally somehow, like she'd failed at the whole extended family thing.

"Okay good. And there's something else. Mark and his family will be joining us for a cookout on Sunday."

"What? Why?" I was ready to lunge, this time prepared to make it hurt.

"Francesca, please. Let this happen. Do it for me. I am begging you." GG had chocolate circles under her eyes and her hands were lumpier than usual.

Logan, who was checking the ends of her hair for any new splits, stopped and cast a worried glance my way.

"Whatever," I took an apple out of the fruit bowl and left the room. First off—I had the George thing on Sunday and secondly, what the hell was happening here? GG was begging me. Begging? Why did it mean so much to her?

From behind me I heard Logan. "Really Ghita, it'll be fine. I'll talk to her."

She followed me outside and all the way to the edge of the lawn.

"Chess?"

"Look Logan, forget it, okay? No offense or anything."

Her arm brushed against mine as we looked out into the roadway.

"I still hate him too, Chessie. Do you know what we talked about the day he was here?"

"What?"

"Polar bears. He was so nervous he started talking about polar bears."

"No way."

She nodded. "Yes way. Do you know how you can tell the difference between a male and female polar bear?"

I looked at her with my eyebrows scrunched together. "Is this a joke?"

"No. For real. It's not so obvious. With all that fur it can sometimes be hard to see. So you watch how they pee. Females pee straight down and males pee off to the side."

I stared at her. My eyebrows stayed bunched up. "He did not. He really did *not* talk to you about the sexual organs of a polar bear."

"Yeah, he did." Her mouth curled at the corner.

"Really?"

"Yes."

That's when Logan and I shared our first laugh at the expense of our father, Mark Madrid, the polar bear advocate and savior.

"Pitiful," I said.

"So anyway, I'm thinking maybe I should give him another chance to do it right this time. Besides, part of me wants to meet the next victim he's got lined up."

"Victim and child," I added.

"For some reason this seems to mean a lot to your grandma."

I tossed the apple across the street and into the neighbors' rhododendron bush. Then I released a sigh and a nod.

*For some reason.*

Logan looped an arm over my shoulder. In that instant I wanted to ask her to stay, though I left that unsaid, too.

★

On the day of Mrs. Delafield's operation, I went to see Doc Abner by myself. He had a red cold sore on the corner of his lip that I couldn't stop staring at. What if he had the herpes virus? I hoped he wouldn't touch me, even if I was too sick that it didn't make a difference. He had a hard time looking me in the eye and stammered when he spoke. They were the classic signs. He was breaking up with me.

"Francesca, I think Dr. Pigeon is more adequately equipped to handle your case. I feel we should consider arranging for more frequent visits with him."

"But he's real far away. I'd rather continue to see you."

"I understand how you feel. However I'm afraid it would be for the best."

I shrugged my shoulders. "I guess so."

"I still want you to come in, perhaps once a month." He was saying we could still be friends.

"Have you told my grandmother?"

"Not yet. I'll give her a call tonight."

"She isn't home. She's away for a couple of days."

"Oh?"

"Stripper convention in Edenville."

Doc Abner folded into his old leather chair. I thought he was going to dribble out the side.

"I'm only kidding. She's at Mrs. Delafield's."

He extended his hand and I shook it in spite of the herpes. From the corner of my eye I saw Mrs. Abner watching as I left. She called a "take care dear" into the air and I gave her a back-handed wave. Meg once told me she caught the Doc and his wife making out on the examining table. I don't know if she made that up. If not it's pretty kinky for such an old couple.

☆

It was a little weird spending the night at home with Logan without GG as a buffer. It was as if my grandmother was the bridge between us. I began to think maybe I was the reason Logan was planning to leave. If I had been nicer or paid more attention to her…maybe then she'd want to stay. I vowed to do what I could to keep her.

She was, after all Wish Number One. I just had to make it stick. If not, what would that mean for the rest of them?

## The Family Madrid

"You don't have to entertain me, Chessie," Logan said on Thursday right after we got back from picking up dinner. She felt like Chinese and we decided to take it to go.

"I'm not. I thought it would be nice to get out of the house tonight, hang out someplace else for a change."

"If you want to," she said. "It's all the same to me."

It wasn't fear that sent me in search of things to do with Logan. It was more like insecurity. I'd slipped through a minor Big S episode earlier in the day and it left me feeling shaky, dehydrated and mildly nauseous. I then called in sick to work, not giving a good hot damn about the Dairy Maid, et al.

Watching Logan, who ate like she'd never had an egg roll in her entire life, made me forget my pain.

"There's the Bowl-n-Bat in Edenville. Might be fun," I suggested.

Meg had asked if we wanted to hit a party at Shelley's. I refused. If my recently acquired sister would be gone so soon, I wanted her all to myself while I still could. Deep down I was scared Johnny and Sara would be there and it was over the top for me. "Or the mall."

Logan lifted a wide sesame noodle into the air with her fingers and dropped it into her mouth. "I think bowling."

"Okay then."

We talked so much that I hardly missed GG who phoned to check in. She said Mrs. Delafield was coming along nicely with the help of a walker and her feisty spirit, whatever that was.

I could tell she was more worried about me than she let on. I wanted to tell her it was good between us. I wanted to tell her how much I loved her. Yet all I could say with Logan right there was "hurry home."

Logan and I skipped plates and ate straight out of the cardboard boxes the food came in. The fortune cookies were waiting in a little wax paper bag stapled closed on one end. Just as soon as we were done with the main course, Logan divvied them up, selecting hers first.

"Once," she said, "I got one of these that said I was going to meet a relative from out of the blue."

"No you didn't."

"Yup," she said with a nod. She was dressed in white from head to toe and looked like a nun I knew from the church, Sister Agatha. She cracked her cookie open with one hand and read, "The recipe for success—dream big and study hard."

"That's probably true." It was my turn next. I opened my cookie half expecting what I'd find. I skimmed the words carelessly at first and then...huh?

"What, Chess?"

"It says, 'The ending is just a backwards beginning.'"

Logan smiled and got up from her chair. I couldn't move. My legs went numb. It had to be a mistake. I looked inside the bag, still on the table. Maybe there was one more cookie, the one that had *my* fortune inside. But it was empty. And all at once, so was I.

Logan was washing her hands at the sink. "Are we going now, or what?"

"Sure, yeah, sure," I replied.

Logan tossed her paper into the top of the trashcan. As soon as I was able, I put mine there too, and walked away without looking back.

★

They were having leagues at the Bowl-n-Bat so we opted for the batting cages. I watched as Logan hit every single ball the machine threw at her.

"Wow, you're good," I told her.

"I was the captain of my school softball team," she reminded me.

"Oh yeah. I forgot. Were you also like their best hitter?"

"I had a solid 290 batting average."

"That's great…I think. Is it?" I asked.

"It's not bad." She smiled. "You want to try now?"

"I guess so. I haven't done this much." I began with a firm disclaimer and proceeded to miss the first six balls in a row. "Okay, I suck. You can go again."

"It helps if you just watch the ball coming at you and imagine it's somebody who makes you real mad. When it's almost in your face you swing away."

"Really?" I asked. "Who did you imagine the ball was?"

"Mark."

So that was it. That was how Logan managed to move past her biting rage at the father who had abandoned her. If Mark Madrid had been half the parent he was supposed to be, Logan might very well have been the captain of the chess team instead.

"Go on," she said, "give it a try."

I was all set to picture my father in his brown plaid shirt and tennis shoes when, out of the corner of my eye, I spotted Johnny Lauten walking past the front desk, his arm draped in ownership over Sara's shoulders. She had her hand in equal ownership in the back pocket of his jeans and they were laughing at some new joke that was all their own.

"Let her rip," I told Logan who pressed the release button on the pitching machine. I hit that ball with a smack that echoed so loud I think the happy couple might have heard. I saw him glance my way and then turn away like he didn't even know me.

"Mark?" Logan asked.

I shook my head. Logan looked past me and over to where Johnny and Sara were standing. "Oh…I see. In that case, you have to keep going."

I hit 12 out of twenty.

★

She introduced herself to me as Anne Darrow Madrid. I knew plenty of people who had three names, although most of them didn't use all three, all the time. I couldn't help but think of her as a one woman legal firm. She even looked the part. Mark's latest lady was nothing like the ones he'd had before. She wasn't the dark, long-haired, bohemian beauty my mother was or the tall, striking, model type like Logan's mom. Anne Darrow Madrid came to our barbeque dinner wearing a pair of crisp cotton trousers with a pressed seam running up the front of each leg. She wore a navy blue collared top and a canary yellow colored sweater tied loosely around her shoulders. It was very possible she came straight from a weekend meeting at the office without stopping to change her clothes. Her auburn hair was cropped closely to her head, in an efficient style that probably required little more than two minutes of brushing once or twice a day. She hadn't bothered to rub any rouge over her trim, freckled cheeks or any lipstick over her pale pink lips. Yet Anne Darrow Madrid wasn't sloppy or careless with her appearance. She had every "I" dotted and every "T" crossed. The wife of Mark Madrid was completely, professionally organized right down to her sensible heels.

GG was more taken with Max. It was hard not to be. I wanted him to be one of those annoying, whiny brats like the ones tired mothers shoved down into highchairs at work. I wanted Max Madrid to be Mark's punishment child—difficult, colicky, with a terminal case of dirty diapers. But he smelled like baby powder and he made those incoherent baby noises people describe as gurgles and coos. And when he was prompted by Anne Darrow Madrid, Max managed a well-rehearsed high five to wow the crowd. To my surprise and minor irritation, Mark Madrid looked like a family man, complete with one sweetly compliant family. I watched my so-called father balance Max on his lap with the greatest of ease. I watched Max, with his red chubby cheeks, freshly grown patch of strawberry blond hair and giant blue eyes look right past the man who, if past performance counts for anything, would end up leaving him in about two-and-a-half years.

Max Madrid spent a good deal of his young time in my backyard staring at me.

"Enjoy it now, kid," I told him from inside my head. "Only don't get too used to your daddy. He won't stay for very long."

Max smiled a drooling, toothless, ignorant grin and I felt sorry for him. He deserved a father for life not a father for now. GG always said that leopards can't change their spots. Mark was as spotted as they came. I wondered why Anne Darrow Madrid, for as smart as she appeared with her neat clothing and proficient looks, hadn't been able to see for herself that one day she'd be left to balance her little boy all alone.

"Chessie, your father has told me so much about you. You too, Logan." Mark's wife swirled her iced tea around in her frosted glass with a clear plastic stir straw GG only used when there was company.

"Really?" I asked, and both Logan and GG snapped their eyes in my direction. They were scared I would say something real, something everybody wanted to say but were too polite to.

"Yes, he's very exited about the prospect of spending time with you girls." Anne Darrow Madrid waited until her husband went to use the bathroom to share this information.

"So you're planning to be here in Missouri for a while?" I asked again.

Logan was holding Max and shifting him from one hip to the other. GG, who had decided to wear her church dress and an extra helping of rose blossom perfume, kept her gaze on my mouth. She was dying to say my birth-I-mean-business name.

"Well…I think your father wanted to be the one to tell you. See we've actually found a place just outside of St. Louis." Mrs. Madrid was smiling. Her teeth were about as white as they could be and still be human teeth.

Mark, in his long khaki shorts and brown sandals and pea green striped shirt, did his best to look casual. Yet his face would not comply. Every muscle around his mouth and nose and eyes steadfastly refused to pretend everything wasn't peculiar, awkward and terrible beneath it all.

"Just outside of St. Louis," I repeated. "Interesting choice." I scanned the yard for my grandmother. She was nowhere to be found. I then fixed my eyes on Mark.

"But it's only temporary, right?"

Mark rose from the webbed lawn chair he was settled in. "Chessie, let's take a walk."

"No, thank you," I said as if he were making more of an offer than a request.

Anne's smile slowly faded until Logan came to deposit Max in her lap. GG was carting trays of condiments around in aimless circles while she studied my face. Her forehead was bright red.

The Madrid's stayed for a little under four hours. During that time Logan and Max bonded the way half-siblings do in a little under four hours. She kept asking me if I cared to hold him, which I did not. I never really got used to small children, and I figured if I dropped him on his head and cracked his skull it might ruin the entire afternoon. GG felt the need to remind me that Max was my brother and how he even looked a bit like me which if I squinted and tilted my head all the way to the left I supposed I could see—a little. But the best part of the day was when Mark sat beside me and took it upon himself to tap my leg in a parental familiar style, like a hello without words. My leg saw fit to remind him that we are *not* that familiar and he immediately chose another chair. Come to think of it, perhaps that wasn't really the best part of the day so much as it was the worst.

He and Logan got on way better. I saw them chatting in the corner of the yard near the vegetable garden. I told myself he was merely arranging for babysitting dates for his son.

It was just before the family Madrid was set to leave that Anne asked one small question. "So how do you like working at the Dairy Maid?"

A ton of bricks fell from the sky and landed on my head. It was Sunday.

Oh my God. George.

## Why the Movie is a Better Choice

He was wearing a pair of black dress pants and a T-shirt that read, "St. Louis Chill" which I presumed to be either an ice cream chain or a pro hockey team which made more sense, though I wouldn't swear to it since I'd never really followed sports. George's hair was brushed into place and wouldn't move. Even the front piece that usually pops up in a troubling arch was suddenly obedient. His eyes breezed over me in my jean shorts and ratty old top as he spoke from behind his front door.

"You could have called."

"George, I'm so, so, sorry. I didn't mean to miss the party, really I didn't."

He was staring down at his feet, at his large shiny black Oxford's. I didn't think he saw much besides a freshly polished pair of dancing shoes for the boy who didn't dance. "So, what happened?" he asked after a hundred minutes of a hundred pound silence.

"It's a long story see my grandmother invited my father and his family for dinner."

George scratched the side of his chin. "I don't understand that."

"It's a whole crazy thing, George. It started with these three wishes—"

"What?"

"Never mind. Look I feel really bad for standing you up. I swear it was unintentional. Can you forgive me?"

He took a full two minutes to respond. His shoulders were

pitched down, his eyes refusing to make direct contact with mine. "Yeah, sure. Thanks for coming by, Chessie," he said, before he took a step back and closed the door. I don't know if it was my imagination, but I thought I saw a tear in his eye. As I drove away I convinced myself it couldn't possibly be so.

☆

Over the next few days I decided to pay closer attention to my half-sister. I felt like I only knew her in the way a person knew a song they hummed because they weren't sure of the words. I figured if she was going to head back to Louisiana soon then maybe I'd start to get better acquainted with the lyrics of Logan Mathews.

I watched her when she shared breakfast with GG and me. She kept her elbows off the table, cleared her plate and always helped with the dishes. She talked about current events enough to sound like an anchorperson for the evening news yet showed a nurturing side like a Florence Nightingale in training. Every now and then she relayed a memory that involved her mother, but she stopped just as quickly. And she never spoke of her aunt or the trouble that brought her to be arrested. It was as if Logan had stepped off the pages of her own life the day she stepped off the bus at Edenville.

She wore no makeup and never fussed with her appearance. Yet I hadn't ever seen her look any less than beautiful.

Her clothes were a lot like mine—clean, careful and not too flashy. Logan seemed confident yet modest, pliable yet solid, rich yet poor. I don't know if I was able to draw any definite conclusions. I heard GG once describe her to somebody as a "nice kid." I guess that was good enough. Logan would leave and I would be able to say that I met my half-sister and she was a nice kid.

A sweet Missouri breeze meandered through the morning. It lifted us out from between our walls and onto the porch with our warm tea.

"Chessie…hellooo?" Logan pulled me back from my thoughts.

"Don't you have to cover the lunch shift today?" GG was staring at me as though I'd temporarily gone missing right before her eyes.

"Yeah, I do." I took to my feet in an instant to head indoors.

"Well, don't forget we're having supper at Mrs. Delafield's tonight," she announced.

"We are?" I asked.

"Didn't I mention? I'm sure I did. Yes, supper at seven thirty. She'd love it if you girls could see fit to be there."

"GG, I have plans later—we both do. We're going to the movies with some friends." This was only half true. I had plans and they were to do anything but be at Mrs. Delafield's at seven thirty.

GG was checking our faces, Logan's and mine. I watched Logan nod along with my excuse like a professional Pinocchio. I imagined until now she'd had very little experience with lying. Until now. Until me. When she went home, her friends would ask her what she learned in Eden's Pond and she'd say, "I learned how to be dishonest."

"Oh that's fine. What do two young chicks need from eating dinner with a couple of old hens? You two go out and enjoy the movies. The popcorn's on me."

"Extra butter," Logan whispered to me.

"Absolutely."

☆

Patty Glick was the prettiest girl I knew with a lazy eye and a lisp. She was also the only girl I knew with a lazy eye and a lisp. I was surprised to see her filling the cone canister, as I was sure I was scheduled to work with George.

"Yeah, he sthwitched out with me," she said, swinging her long blonde ponytail behind her as she opened a fresh package of burger buns.

"Did he ask or did you?"

"Howth that?"

"Did George ask to switch out or did you?" I struggled to tie my apron and Patty took hold of it to help me.

"He did," she answered and then drew the strings extra tight as if to drive the point home.

I knew right then George was avoiding me. "Did he say why? Did he say why he needed to take off?"

Patty kept moving across the floor as though her chores were being timed. "No, but that was thomthing about that fight with Cole Harris, huh?"

"Cole Harris is a complete turd."

"Yeah, and to think George was only defending your thithter."

I trailed her as she went into the storeroom for a stack of fry cups.

"Did you say he was defending my sister?"

"Uh-huh. Cole was making some nathty comments about her and you, and George was thticking up for you both. He wound up getting clobbered pretty good though. Poor Georgie. He'th kind of thweet, don't ya think?"

Yes. I did. Dammit.

"Patty, are you sure that's what happened?" I had to stop her from flitting away. I grabbed her by the arm. "Are you totally positive?"

"Yeah, I am. Jeez Cheth, don't freak out or anything."

"I'm not freaking out. I had no idea what happened," I said, and she was already out of the room when I added, "He wouldn't tell me. He didn't want me to know." I thought about how I once assumed George was a boy who didn't stand for anything other than clean floors. Yet he had the nerve to stand up for me when I could barely muster up enough to even be seen with him outside of the Dairy Maid.

I slithered on my belly on the grimy ground back to my post. I was the lowest form of life in that moment. And George was suddenly my unlikely hero.

★

"Sold out," Logan sighed. "All the good ones are sold out." There wasn't much to do on a rainy Wednesday night in Eden's Pond therefore the movie theatre was usually real crowded. We wanted to see something between animated and pornographic. That left a screen adaptation of some sappy musical that Logan said she recognized or an alien comes to earth in the body of a priest thing.

"I can't believe they're both sold out!" Logan said again.

"You want to just get a big bucket of popcorn and head home? It doesn't matter, GG's already at Mrs. Delafield's now anyway."

So we ordered the popcorn, extra butter, and two boxes of chocolate covered peanuts to go. We discussed whether or not we'd tell GG the truth about not actually seeing a movie. Logan thought it wouldn't matter as long as we'd tried to. I told her about George sticking up for us with Cole Harris. I could say things to her I would normally censor around Meg. It was a feeling of freedom that was sort of cool.

"George sounds like a nice guy," she said.

"Yeah, I guess he is."

"Maybe he likes you."

I turned the corner onto my street and then shook my head. "God no! We work together that's all…"

"Chess, look." Logan pointed out what I had just seen for myself, the car parked next to the old oak tree in front of our place. The car with the out of state plates, the one Mark was driving when he came to visit.

"What is *he* doing here?" I asked. And why hadn't GG mentioned he was coming?

"I thought Ghita was over at her friend's house having dinner." Logan fidgeted with her seat belt as if she planned to break free and take one of her runs right then.

"I thought so too." I pulled over across the road. I didn't want to make my presence known.

"Maybe she wanted to have her own chance to speak to him," Logan suggested in an urgent whisper.

I shook my head. "No. This isn't about her—it's about me. Come on."

"Chessie—"

"Be as quiet as you can and follow me. If I know my grandmother, and I do, she's got him in the dining room. She only entertains her comfortable guests in the kitchen. Anything else takes place in there. It's her formal room for things that mean business. That's where they'll be. We can duck down behind the window and listen in." I began to tiptoe across the pavement and she followed, lagging a bit behind.

"Chessie, we shouldn't. It's not right. Maybe it's private stuff they're talking about, stuff we shouldn't know."

I knew exactly what they were discussing. I also knew it was a subject I preferred Logan not to overhear. Still I had to confirm a hunch I had since the afternoon of the barbeque dinner.

"Logan, there is something going on in that house, and I need to know what it is."

"Okay, well, if you're going to be sneaky, at least do it right. Move your car up a bit or they'll liable to notice it out here."

"Good point," I said, and she followed as I hid the car three houses away and behind a row of freshly trimmed arborvitaes. We crept like two Mata Hari's behind the house and over to the dining room window, which was open a good five inches. GG loved the smell of fresh summer rain, which had started up again, in time to drown out the sound of our feet on the ground below. We took our stations one on either side of the window while we pressed our bodies up against the siding. I could hear their voices, muffled at first. GG was straining at her words, choosing them slowly and carefully.

"I know she's headstrong… Chessie has every reason to be, Mark. She'll fight this so it's up to us to make sure it works."

"I'll do whatever it takes. We have a room all ready for her."

Logan listened with her eyes up toward the dark stormy sky while I listened with mine pinned on the wet dirt below.

"We have one for Logan, too," Mark continued.

"I'll need some time to get Chessie used to the notion. She's been hurting for so long."

I heard no reply, only the clinking of silverware against the china she kept in the corner cupboard. It was GG who spoke again. "Eventually I know she'll recognize it's for her own good."

I hadn't realized my hands were balled in two fists at my side or that Logan wasn't looking up anymore. She was looking at me.

Mark's voice was tight. "I want to be there for her, to help her through this as much as I can. Anne knows some people at the hospital, if it comes to that."

"She's done so well. The doctors are amazed. God has been kind." In that instant my heart dropped out of its spot in my chest and plummeted to my feet. Maybe GG had already told Logan, made her promise never to tell. Maybe GG had needed a shoulder for leaning and Logan's was just right. It didn't matter now, either way.

In that instant my sister took my hand. It was then she knew I was going to die.

## Pink Nails

Meg was filing her nails and getting them ready for a coat of black nail polish.

We were in her room, and she alternated between fussing over her fingers and my hair. She kept saying she wished she'd never cut all hers off. I didn't mention anything about my grandmother's little scheme. None of it would make any sense to her anyhow. It hardly made any sense to me. The only logical explanation was that GG must have gone stark raving mad. If she thought for five seconds that I'd ever live with Mark Madrid in St. Louis she was quite simply out of her mind.

"Did I tell you Johnny is moving out?"

"No. Is he?" I hadn't seen much of Meg's big brother lately, and I was just as relieved not to. I wasn't able to erase the mental image of his naked body from my mind; it appeared at the most inopportune moments like while I was washing the dishes or brushing my teeth.

"Yeah. He says he's had enough of being bossed around by my folks. What he really means is he wants to be able to have as much sex with as many girls as he can without getting into trouble." Meg was braiding my hair even though I hated braids.

"So where is he moving to?" I tried to sound casual, not as interested as I was.

"Some stupid one room apartment in Edenville, above a pet shop. I guess he doesn't care about the noise. I guess he figures he'll be able to drown out the animals and they won't complain about him either."

"Wow. So when?"

"He's pretty much all packed up. I think by next week. It'll be nicer here without him. My mother swears he'll have somebody pregnant one of these days, and the last thing we need is a screaming kid hanging around. Hey, I'll do your nails if you like."

"With that?" I glanced at her choice and made a sour face.

"Pink is better?"

"Pink is better."

I liked hanging out at Meg's. I was a girl with pink nails at Meg's. Ever since Logan found out about the Big S she'd hovered around me as if she were waiting for me to keel over. She hadn't asked many questions, not to me. I suspect she and GG were talking up a storm as soon as I left. And speaking of leaving, Logan wasn't. She'd said it once, about living with her friend in Louisiana. But she hadn't mentioned it again. I wondered if her plans had changed. Was she worried about me too, now that she officially knew the deal? I didn't want to be the person everybody felt bad for. It was torture for me to think about the faces of the people who would hear the news and offer me one of those short, straight smiles like Doc Abner's done a hundred times. Only one person wouldn't pity me because he was 150% totally focused on himself.

"You feel like getting some ice cream?" I asked Meg who had just finished painting her own nails.

"Right now? I'll smudge."

"That's okay. I'll go and get it and bring it back."

"Sure. I'll take butter pecan…no, make it a mint chocolate chip with colored sprinkles. Your treat, right?"

Meg never had money, or she pretended not to. "Yeah, my treat."

"Cool. Go, hurry up."

"I will," I said and I left her there with her black fingertips and her mouth full of extra saliva. The truth is I had an agenda, a plan of distraction with a capital D. I was still me, still the girl with two good fortunes and four wishes.

I'd heard him moving around downstairs, and knew he'd be

there, in the living room, staring at the television screen. Johnny barely looked my way as I stood in the doorway.

"What's up?" he asked.

"I'm going for ice cream. Do you want any?"

"Umm…okay. Get me a cup of raspberry vanilla."

"All right. Hey, do you want to come with me?" I mustered a canned smile.

This time he looked me over. "What for?"

"I don't know."

He took a minute to survey me with my braids and my overall shorts. "Cute look."

I shrugged. "So?"

"Hang on. I'll go." He got up on his feet. "Give me a sec," he told me and disappeared for a minute before he joined me in my car. "I need a smoke break. How about you?" he asked, as I took off with him lighting a joint.

"Not while I'm driving. I hear you're moving out."

"Yeah. I can't take their shit anymore. I need my space, you know? Well maybe you don't know."

"No, I do," I said.

"You want to see my new place?" He began eyeing me the same way he did the night at the lake.

"I thought you don't move in until next week."

"I don't, but I have the key," he pulled it out of the front pocket of his jeans and dangled it in the air, back and forth as though trying to hypnotize me. Maybe he already had.

"Where is it?"

"About five blocks from the ice cream shop."

I wasn't sure what to say. I was afraid again all at once, afraid to go and afraid not to. I was a baby if I didn't. What was I if I did?

"Well?" He blew a steady stream of smoke into the air followed by a perfectly round white ring.

"I'll go."

"Then we'll do that first."

I was sure I'd chosen wrong. Meg would say so. Logan would

too. GG would remind me that Johnny had the devil in his details and probably in his brand new apartment-to-be. But Meg wasn't there, and Logan was with GG and her big St. Louis plans.

I'd been feeling mad at the world and at everything that was supposed to be right and really wasn't. I began to wonder if there was one pivotal moment in a person's life when things turned forever backwards or inside out or both. Down meant up, dark was light. Wrong became the new right. My moment had snuck up on me when I was busy believing that bad was bad and good was good and that was that. And now I had to rearrange my thinking if I were going to survive.

Johnny's apartment looked a lot like a room with three doors if you counted the one we came in from. The other one was for the bathroom and the third for a small closet to keep a coat or some towels, I guess. I didn't mention that his bedroom at Meg's house was twice the size. He seemed to like the windows most of all, which I thought was strange since at home he had cardboard over his window.

"Where's the kitchen?" I asked, to which pointed behind me toward the corner of the room. A metal framed desktop with a sink stuck right through it and a hotplate plugged in along the side was crammed against the wall. The refrigerator was clearly meant for people who were less than three feet tall and was tucked down beneath the desk.

"Oh, yeah. It's nice."

"Whatever. I don't plan on cooking anything here anyhow. The best thing is it's all mine. I can walk around here with my ass hanging out all day if I want to."

"And Sara can sleep over anytime." I didn't know what I was saying. The words were out, the ridiculous words were out of my mouth and he'd heard them.

"Hell *anyone* can," he said. It was his way of inviting me to be anyone.

"Still she's your girlfriend again so it should be *her*, right?"

Johnny took one step closer to me and I took one back.

"Where do you get your ideas, Chessie? Does stuff always have to add up to you?"

"What?" I didn't follow what he meant. I moved in closer to him.

He was so near I could smell the faintest hint of stale cigarettes and cherry Coke in the air just outside his mouth. "Do you see a wedding ring on my finger?"

"No, but—"

"Don't you think it's possible to like more than one person at a time?"

It's obvious he had forgotten about the history of my family. Did I think it was possible? I thought it was painfully possible.

"Of course it is." I backed up again. "Still, that doesn't make it okay."

Johnny's hands were on top of my arms. "Okay or not…it happens."

His lips were waiting for mine, which went of their own accord. Kissing him was good and bad; two plus two equals five. Stuff in my world *never* added up.

"Do you like me?" he whispered behind my braid and into my left ear.

I nodded, half hoping he didn't see my reply. It didn't matter. He knew the answer anyway. And in that moment I knew it too. It was a crazy weird moment—one where I'd forgotten about Meg and her ice cream and Mark Madrid and his family and most of all I forgot in that weird moment about Doc Abner and Dr. Pigeon and the Big S.

✯

GG was collecting basil leaves from the garden against the back fence, where the stalks waved to the tiny brown sparrows nesting in the evergreen towering overhead. She called to me to bring her a basket from the kitchen cupboard, which was her flimsy way of asking me to be with her. It was a sultry morning after—after I'd been with Johnny and his warm mouth on mine. I'd slipped into a pair of short-shorts and flip-flops, a tank top and my easiest up-do and sauntered out to her, all the while staring down at my pink fingertips.

My grandmother's nails were unpolished and yellow stained on the edges. The veins in her hands were twisted into a tangle of knots. "Chessie, you do know that you are my dearest, dearest girl. You do know that, don't you?"

I handed the basket over to her. "Yes, I know."

"Yet you feel as though I've betrayed you. That would be the same as me betraying my very own heart."

I plucked the dark green pungent leaves off the vines. "GG, how can you ever expect me to spend my days under the same roof as Mark? After all he's done; after all he hasn't done. How?"

My grandmother stopped and turned to me. "Francesca, your mother once made a request of me. She asked that if anything ever happened to her I'd see to it you and your father reunite. I never wanted to do it and yet, I can't ignore her plea. Not anymore. I will sell my soul to the devil, I'll spend my eternity in his heated clutch if it means you'll outlive me."

I took a deep sigh and checked the sky above for a read of the sun. It was such a beautiful sight. I never wanted to let it go. I never wanted to let her go. I leaned into her shoulder and whispered, "I love you, too."

## All Things Provisional

Logan received a letter on Monday morning. Not a special delivery or anything, but I think it was from her aunt in jail, so maybe it was sort of special in that she'd never gotten one before. GG handed it to Logan who took it into the sewing room and closed the door. We didn't see her again for an hour, and then when she came out she looked the way she did after she took one of her runs, all tousled and flushed.

"Is everything all right, Logan?" GG asked.

"Yes. I was accepted into a college back home. They've offered me a full scholarship," she said, as if it was no big deal.

GG smiled. "That's wonderful. It's an honor."

"Wow. That's great. Which school?" I asked.

"Tulane."

I'd heard of it, and I knew it was a fancy university. Logan made it sound like kindergarten.

"I'm pretty sure that's a good school," I told her.

She shrugged and reached for a banana.

"Don't you want to go?" GG was piling a small stack of folded tissues into her handbag.

"My aunt thinks I should... I don't know."

"Logan, this is an opportunity of a lifetime." My grandmother believed education was the next nearest thing to religion. Refusing to learn, for free, was like refusing an audience with the pope.

"I suppose. Although then I'll have to leave here sooner than I planned." Logan drew back the smooth yellow peel.

GG stopped her tissue duty and looked Logan straight in the eyes. "Sweetheart, you are always welcome here. We'll miss you terribly. However, your aunt is right. You should go to college and get a degree. You owe it to your mind."

Logan smiled at GG but wouldn't look at me. "My aunt sent me money for a bus ticket. Arrangements have been made for me to stay with my friend until school starts. Aunt Vicky wants me to thank you for your grace and hospitality."

"It was our pleasure, Logan. Please remember you're a part of this family too now, no matter where you live." GG wrapped her arms around Logan's shoulders, only for a minute, to accentuate her point. I think both of them wanted to cry yet neither one did. I felt something stir inside, though I wasn't sure what it was. When you're a person with a long history of people frequently leaving your life, you adjust to the notion way before it actually happens. From the onset, Logan was temporary. She was a sister for the time being, a friend for the moment and a round-trip relation. She was a childhood wish that somehow came true. And so it was that Temporary Logan was to fulfill her obligatory slot in the realm of all things provisional.

"It'll be awesome, Logan," I said to sum it all up. She gave me a look. I think she wanted to tell me that she was no longer prepared to be a fleeting star in the story of my life.

"You think?" she asked.

"I do. In fact, I know a kid who goes to Tulane. He's real smart too."

"Thanks, Chessie."

We left it at that until GG was safely out of the house. Then Logan put her letter and her smile away and sat down across from me in the yard where I was enjoying the lack of humidity and a soft, stirring wind in the quiet early afternoon.

"It doesn't feel right for me to go. Not anymore." She was wearing the same clothes she wore on the day of her arrival. Maybe it was her boomerang outfit. Maybe she would be on the last bus out of Edenville tonight.

"Because of my being sick?"

"Yes."

"Do you think I won't be sick anymore if you stay?" I wasn't trying to be mean. I just wondered whether Logan really imagined herself to be that important.

"It doesn't feel like I'd be doing the right thing, that's all."

"You're doing the exact right thing."

"Well, I was thinking I could wait until the spring semester, perhaps spend the fall and winter here with you."

I watched that wind swirl around her head, spinning her hair around like a lasso. I knew she was worried about me and it gave me a sense of sisterhood that I never imagined I'd know.

"It's probably better if you start now, seeing as how they're willing to give you all that money. I'll be all right. Nothing is going to happen here that I can't handle."

She fiddled with fixing herself up, pushing her hair behind her ears a few times and then straightening her shoulders. "Chess, I want you to know I liked being here with you and Ghita. I'm not sure, but it was starting to feel like things with Mark were going somewhere too. If I'm stepping out of all of that by leaving, then I'll be sorry I did."

She was desperately scared to let it go. Maybe then it would be like it never even happened. Life can be like that sometimes. And she knew it as well as I did.

"We'll stay in touch. I promise," I told her.

She nodded and stood up. Endings are weird in that they turn up so quickly you hardly see them coming. As she turned to go inside, I felt the breeze brush my face.

"Logan? I liked having you here too."

I didn't look back at her, yet I could tell she was smiling. Then I remembered the last fortune cookie with the mixed message about endings and beginnings. Perhaps it had been referring to Logan and me and not a prelude to something more cryptic. Either way I soothed a small ache in the core of my chest, not an episode at all but maybe a little tear in the lining of my heart.

✭

Three days later, on Thursday at six p.m., GG, Logan and I took a quiet drive to the Edenville bus station. GG wished Logan a safe journey and sent her off with a "Godspeed" and a hug. As for me, I walked Logan over to the depot, afraid to hug her. Afraid not to. In that moment I wanted to tell her not to leave. The words were on my tongue, and they tasted rotten sitting there unsaid. Suddenly there were so many of them. I held them in with all my might. Logan, I won't forget how you helped me into the house the night I got locked out and how you didn't judge the circumstances. I won't forget when we went to the bowling alley, and you taught me how to swing a bat. I was just learning how it feels to have a half-sister and it felt half-good. I swallowed them all, swallowed hard and fast and down they went. We left one another with a toothless grin.

"I'll call you," she promised.

"We'll talk soon," I said.

GG and I stared out of opposite windows on the way home. The sun seemed misplaced with its late day bright yellow smile. Maybe, instead, for just that hour, the sky should have been gray.

✭

George has succeeded in dodging me for almost two weeks, switching his schedule with anybody he could to avoid working with me. He might have pulled it off tonight too, except I'd decided enough was enough, and enacted a switch of my own with Patty, who was supposed to be on duty with him from four to nine. Right after he arrived I registered the look of surprise and disappointment on his face. I followed him into the back room where he arranged his things on the employee shelf without so much as a hello.

"What's up, George? It's been a while."

"It's been two weeks, Chessie," he told me with his face pointed down at the floor.

"I know. George, are you mad at me? About the dinner thing? Because I'm sorry about that. That's why I came over to your house that night, to say I was sorry."

"I know. I guess it feels weird to me."

It was five minutes to four. I doubted I could even begin to explain things quickly enough to make it right before we had to go up front and pedal slop.

"George…listen, I didn't plan on standing you up. It wasn't my intention at all. I *had* to see my family for my grandmother's sake. If I could tell you the whole story I would, but I can't. I really *did* want to go to that dinner with you. And you could at least look at a person when they're trying to apologize."

He turned and squared a set of limp eyelids with mine. His mouth hung off the bottom of his face. I guessed then that he'd been through a thing like that before in his life, being disappointed by a girl. Being hurt by a girl.

"Is there anything I can do to make it up to you? Anything at all, within reason of course. Name it, and I will."

"What's within reason?" he asked.

"Well, I won't do anything wacky or illegal or anything that involves me removing my clothes. And I'll work for you any time you need me to."

He stared at me. "Do me a favor, Chessie. Be decent. That's all. Be a decent person to me, and I'll do the same to you."

"Sure. Okay, decent."

He straightened his shoulders as he walked away. He appeared taller to me than he'd ever looked before. Maybe he grew, or I was shrinking. Did being indecent make you smaller?

I watched George as he cooked and served and cleaned and worked the register. I imagined maybe they'd make him manager one day. He was better at it than I was and the customers liked him more. He acted like he didn't hate being there—like it wasn't the biggest drag in the world which it was, if you ask me. I waited until a rush of people had come and gone and things got quiet before I decided to talk to him again.

"George?"

"Yeah."

"I heard about the fight you had with Cole Harris."

"So?"

"I heard what it was about."

"You did?"

I nodded. We were alone behind the counter, and I was spilling old cooking grease out of the deep fryer.

"It was nothing."

"No, it was something. Why did you do that? Why did you defend me?"

"I didn't."

"Yes, you did. Why?"

He pulled the hair out of his eyes and leveled them at me. "Isn't it obvious?"

I shook a brand new sensation, one that tugged at my consciousness, one that suggested George had a very different notion of our friendship. "It was nice of you to do that, George."

I offered him a smile and then he was gone.

## Little Bad Apples

It became the new normal. The episodes came, usually at some convenient moment when there was nothing else to do. Yet when I was with Johnny they never showed up. When I was with him I was healthy and sexy. We were cat and mouse and I was quickly becoming more of a big, fat liar than I'd ever been in my life. This time I was lying to my grandmother and when the guilt crept in I was able to quiet it with reminding my morals that GG had been keeping things from me, too. Secrets with Mark. Even if they were meant for my own good, it was still pretty despicable.

I left the house more and more with a fake destination story, mostly making them up right there on the spot, as I grabbed my keys and headed for the door. If GG asked, I would tell her I was going to the library, to the mall, to the bowling alley, to a friend's, to work even when I wasn't on the schedule, and once I told her I was going to the gym, although I didn't know if there was one anywhere nearby. To tell her I was going to Johnny's apartment would mean to suffer the certain lecture she'd be launching which would begin with, "Francesca, what *are* you thinking?"

I didn't even know how it started—but it did. I wound up in Johnny's place after he and his couch and bed moved in. And then I wound up on his couch and bed. I let him be my first time. And seriously, I didn't think sex was all they made it out to be. I mean so many people obsessed over it, wrote songs about it, cried for it, killed for it and yet I'm pretty sure I thought it was just okay.

I wasn't his girlfriend. Usually we sat around and watched

his 13-inch TV until he started to feel like messing around. Sometimes he smoked pot and I smoked with him. Sometimes I didn't. Sometimes I thought he could love me. Sometimes I didn't. The worst of it was when Sara called, and I was there and she didn't know it. He shushed me and talked to her like he forgot I existed. And then he'd hang up and remember I did, and tell me some stupid joke to lighten the mood. He didn't forget to unhook my bra or unzip his fly. Once or twice he forgot to use protection. Meg was completely in the dark. Actually that wasn't entirely true. Meg thought she knew her brother was up to no good, however she was in the dark that the no good part was *me*. We had this exact conversation one night on the telephone.

Me—"So what's up?"

Her—"Not much. Sara's here. She's crying."

Me—"Really? Why?" *I was cringing since she couldn't see my face.*

Her—"She thinks Johnny is fooling around with some slut."

Me—*Cringing again, this time, a really big one.* "That's too bad."

So it was official. I was some slut. I was some sick slut. In spite of this, perhaps in spite of everything I gathered my things and my latest faux destination to go and be with him again. GG was sitting in the living room, an open magazine in her lap, her glasses riding way down on her nose.

"Are you going out, Chessie?"

"I am."

"Where abouts?"

"To meet a girl I know from the Dairy Maid. We're going to hang out at her house for a while."

"What's her name?" She hadn't looked at me yet.

"Lindsay." Lindsay was a totally fictional person.

"Lindsay what?"

"Miller."

"So she works at the Dairy Maid then?"

"No. She just comes in there to eat and we talk."

"Where does she live?" GG's eyes were skimming the pages below and not skimming mine.

"In Edenville, River Place. I won't be late." I jostled my keys to signal an end to the inquisition.

And then she looked up at me, at last. "All right, sweetheart. Be careful."

"I will, thanks GG."

I was nearly out the door when I heard her voice again. "Chessie?"

"Hmm?"

She didn't speak until she had my complete attention. "Live a life you can be proud of."

I wasn't sure what to say so I said thank you, and ran to my car. My car ran to Johnny's apartment, almost as if on autopilot. I knocked on the door, four sets of two taps, before he answered.

He didn't step aside right away. "Where are you parked?"

"Right downstairs on the street."

"I don't really care, but I get the feeling maybe Sara's thinking about doing a drive-by or even a drop-by."

"Maybe I'll go home then." I kept hearing GG's parting message in my head, and it had started to change my mood.

"No, hey." Johnny reached out and pulled me in to him. "I was just dreaming about you." His mouth landed against mine. I became Rubber Girl with no backbone.

"You were?"

"Uh-huh. Why don't you move your car around the block into the bank parking lot?"

"Really?"

"Oh yeah." He cooed, making me think I was special again.

So I did. I hid my car in the far left corner of the bank parking lot behind an old white delivery van for some seafood restaurant. I could smell cigar smoke. I could hear my grandmother. *Live a life you can be proud of.* I ignored both her and the ghost of Mr. Delafield. Johnny was dreaming about *me.* I had to go. I rushed to his arms. They seemed eager at first, even gentle as they kept me so close it was hard to tell where he ended and I began. I was in my very own romance novel. I was living my own life-long fantasy. I felt wanted, deeply, intensely desired for a whole fifteen minutes. It was intoxicating, and then all at once it was over. Things went cold. He shot for the bathroom and peed with the door open. I combed my hair and was angry at myself for not having lip gloss with me. When he came back I imagined he'd say something sweet and generous. *You're great, Chessie. I'm falling for you.*

"Yo Chess, want a beer?"

A car door banged closed on the road below. Johnny went for the window and stuck his finger through the slats of the blind.

"Shit," he said like he was bored silly.

"What? Who is it? Is it Sara?"

"And Meg."

"Oh my God! What do I do? They can't find me here—they can't!"

"Easy, sweetie. Take it easy. I'll get rid of them. You wait in the bathroom."

"Oh my God!" My feet became fused with the floor. He pushed me along, shoving me into the small room and closing the door in my face.

It was either going to be the thing that broke me or the thing that almost did. I fought an urge to cry and then an urge to cough or sneeze or make some noise that would announce me. I demanded my body to be as still as it had ever been. *No tears!*

As I crouched in the shower stall of Johnny Lauten's bathroom, it dawned on me that apple trees grow little apples. It occurred to me that perhaps I had inherited the same gene of disloyalty my father had. Was I a chip off the old Mark Madrid, no one woman is ever enough to bother being faithful to, block? Was I a liar, a cheater and a thief of hearts? Was I doomed to repeat the sins of my father?

Two tears slid down my cheeks. My throat tightened. My fingers began to tingle as if they'd been plunged into a bucket of ice water. My chest was heavy, anchored with an invisible vest of lead. The Big S managed to find me, even in my oh-so-clever hiding place. I scooped up into a tight, tiny ball, huddling close against myself as my head began to vibrate. Silently I called out for my mother, then my grandmother, then Logan. For five minutes I thought I would spend the final moments of my life trapped in Johnny's bathroom. I thought my last smell would be that of the mildew growing on the ceiling above my head.

But then the pain went away. I straightened my spine and took in the gift of my own breath. My knees were wet. There were puckered dots on my calves from the bath mat I was kneeling on. His voice from inside was muffled, though Meg's was crystal clear.

"The least thing you could do is talk to her. She doesn't even want to come up here, she's *that* upset."

Johnny said either "I don't know why" or "I've seen her cry" to which Meg wielded her most serious tone.

"If you're screwing around then end it with Sara once and for all. It's the only decent thing to do. And this place is gross. It smells like a hamster cage."

This time I heard him clearly too. "I am *not* screwing around, but if she needs me to talk to her I will. And I like hamsters."

The footsteps got smaller and smaller until I heard the outside door smack shut. He'd gone to console her. He would look at her with his sweetest look, hold her hand, touch her cheek and open his mouth to croon a bold face lie she would believe because she loved him and she wanted to. If I were not there he would probably bring her up to his bed to convince her in the way he did best. It killed me not seeing for myself what was going on. Yet I was lulled by the thought that he was doing it for me—to protect me from the consequences of my actions, of his actions with me. He didn't care about being unfaithful to Sara. He didn't care if Meg knew who he was sleeping with. Yet he knew that I did, so I justified his being down there with her in that it was some warped version of heroism on my behalf.

Johnny was gone so long I began to feel like a soggy pretzel, all bent and twisted. With each second that droned by, with each impossible measure of time I imagined he was doing to her what he'd just did to me, right there in the car, Meg's or hers, with Meg standing guard. I envisioned any minute now, someone would burst through the door. Maybe Meg would have to use the bathroom. Maybe I'd be in there when she came in to sit on the toilet, and she wouldn't know because I was hiding behind the red plastic curtain which he found here when he moved in. After what felt like four years, the apartment door opened and then closed. *Bang.*

"It's okay. They're gone," he shouted.

"What happened? What took so long?" I asked as I emerged with my shaky bath-mat legs.

"She was all freaked out. She was like, 'let's break up,' and stuff like that. And Meg kept sticking her giant nose into it."

"So did you guys break up for real?"

"Nah. Sara's too addicted to me. She'll never let it happen."

"Then what?" I was mad. He should be mine now. After all we'd done together. He should have told her it was over, and then he could be with me without all the hiding and lies.

"Look don't *you* start too. I had enough crap with those two!" He sauntered over to his tiny refrigerator and pulled out a Coors. "Damn. I only have two left. Let's take a ride to the store. I need to get some more."

"Johnny."

"C'mon, Chessie. Forget about it, okay?"

"I want to know what you told her."

"It doesn't matter. I got rid of them, for *you.* Now let's go."

He snatched his car keys and his wallet, and I followed him outside. It didn't dawn on me that they might be watching from behind some building nearby. All I could focus on was how Johnny thought he did me this huge favor.

"Are you coming or what?" His voice was sharp at the edges.

"I don't know why you can't tell me what you said to her. I think I should know where you two stand."

We'd reached his car and he waited there, his hands on the rooftop, his brows pinched tight, his lips in a scowl. "Dammit, Chessie. You are one sure pill of a girl, you know that? I had to jump through hoops to keep her from coming upstairs. Do you get that? And all you want to do is bug the shit out of me! I jumped through Goddamn hoops!" When Johnny yelled a vein in his temple inflated till it looked about to pop.

"Gee, I suppose if you jumped through hoops I should say thank you, huh?" I kept my tone soft, sweet and quiet.

"At the very least."

"Well, I won't! You can get your own beer. I'm going home."

"Whatever. If you think I give a rat's ass, you're dead stinkin' wrong. Go home. You'll be back. You're exactly like all the others." Johnny opened the door and got inside. He wasn't scowling anymore. In an instant he was smiling. He didn't wait for me to move away from the car before he threw it in reverse and took off. I watched him turn the corner and kept watching until he was out of sight.

As I walked over to where I'd ditched the Shadow, I asked the universe to help me prove him wrong. In that moment I didn't ever want to come here again. Right then I wanted to hate his guts and tell Meg she was right all along about everything.

I wanted to un-wish Johnny Lauten, un-wish every thought I'd ever had about him.

I would have been better off wishless.

## Orange Ducks

On the drive home I thought about Logan and what she might say if she were still in the sewing room reading a book about European poets and taking notes about the lines she liked best. She'd surely tell me to forget all about Johnny, that love wasn't supposed to make you feel so miserable inside. My mother might tell me so too. Except, did she even know that? After all, she'd fallen in love with the one man destined to make her life a study in romantic frustration.

I thought about the time my mother took me to see the planes take off and land at the Joplin regional airport. I was about ten years old and it was just her and me. She knew a guy that worked there, so we went inside. He gave me a pin, a small set of airplane wings, which he carefully secured to the collar of my shirt. I remember thinking how nice that man was, how he seemed to lift my mom and hold her with his eyes. It occurred to me afterward that perhaps they'd been dating; perhaps he was somebody who might have actually been good for her. If she'd had the chance, I was sure Mom would have discovered the right love in the arms of the right person. That man, whose name I couldn't recall, had rested his open hand on top of my head, which made my mom smile. She'd hugged him as a way of saying thank you. I never saw him again. That one small event kept me convinced there were boys in this universe capable of kindness. Not like Cole Harris or Mark Madrid or Johnny Lauten. Would I ever know one? Would I know only one?

Was George one?

I took my time moving from the Shadow to the porch. Disappointment kept my legs weighted down. The Big S kept my hopes weighted down. Love kept my heart there.

"I want to know why, God? Why me?" I called out into the air. "Why? WHY?"

"Francesca." GG's voice came from behind me where she was standing on the top step wearing a look of sheer fright.

"Sweetheart?"

I crumpled down onto the stair, holding my head in my palms. "Are there good men in this world?"

GG took a minute or so to get situated beside me. I'd never seen her sit anyplace that wasn't specifically designed for sitting. She gathered my hair from my shoulders and collected the loose strands down the center of my back. Her very touch was soothing and sad at the same time. "There are great men in this world. My Raymond, he was a great man. Sometimes you have to sort through them, like melons, to find the one that's ripe. And sometimes they look good on the outside but when you cut them open they're sour. It might take a while. It's romance's way of teaching us patience."

"What if you don't have a while?"

My grandmother didn't answer. She just played with my hair with fingers shaped like bent straw. "Your mother loved your hair. She was always putting it in little pigtails and bows. Did you know you were born with a full head? The only baby in the hospital nursery that didn't need one of those tiny knit caps. Your mom used to say you were a beautician's dream."

I smiled even though she couldn't see it.

"Have I ever mentioned how proud I am of you?"

"I don't know. Probably." I was talking down into the splintered wood.

"Well I am exquisitely proud. I know you are capable of anything. You're so, so strong...like your mom."

I finally faced her. "GG, if it wasn't for Mark, you might still have her. We both would. Don't you hate him for that?"

"If it wasn't for him, I might not have you. Like it or not Chessie, he is the man my daughter fell in love with. Like it or not, she chose to start a family with him. *You* came from that choice. *You* came from her love for him. How can I hate him when he gave me you?"

I threw my arms around her neck. Safety was there in the soft folds of her skin, in the familiar lemony scent of her clothes. "What can I do?"

She held me close. "I want you to get to a place where you can stand him. I want you to try. Do it for your mother, Chessie. It's what she wanted."

I told her I would, for Mom's sake. Then while I was in a giving mood my grandmother made her next request. "He wants to have dinner with you tomorrow night. Alone, the two of you."

"Like a date?"

"No silly. Not like a date. Like dinner."

"Where?"

"I don't know. Does it matter?"

"I guess not. I'll go. If it will make you happy, then I'll go, anyplace but Chinese."

GG rested her forehead against mine. In that instant I let it all go—Johnny and his bad love and the melons I may or may not get the chance to cut open. I melted into her, GG and me, one and the same.

✫

It was a lamb's wool sky, bumpy and white and lit from behind. I watched the window and then the mirror and then the window once more. My reflection was way too sweet and compliant, far too forgiving. I dressed in black, to attempt to express my true feelings. I wanted to be obvious, like a storm, like a thicket of steel gray clouds above.

Yet I was vague, like that sheepskin overhead. I pulled my hair into a tight bun and refused a smile for fear a dimple might make me seem charming.

At 6:45 p.m. Mark picked me up, arriving in the same minivan as when he brought his family over. There were Cheerio crumbs on the floor and an infant car seat in back with a big stain on the arm. He was wearing a tan golf shirt and black jeans. One side of his collar was up and the other was down. He had slimy looking goop in his hair.

"Sorry about the mess. I call this Annie's mothermobile." This was his icebreaker.

"So you're saying mothers can't keep a clean car?"

He smiled, although I didn't get that he was particularly pleased about anything. "Maybe it's the babies that can't keep a clean car!" he suggested.

I think it was his attempt at humor. I didn't laugh.

"Where are we going?" I asked, with a mouth full of chewing gum I smacked loudly between my lips.

"I found this lovely little place about thirty minutes from here. They serve an orange duck to die for."

"Orange what?"

"Orange duck. Well, they serve plenty of other things too, if that doesn't appeal to you."

"It sounds disgusting. I would never, ever eat a duck."

Mark nodded. "I understand. I felt that way too when I was your age. Your tastes can change as time passes."

"I don't care if my tastes change. I will *never, ever* eat a duck."

"You eat chicken, don't you?"

I had my fingers wrapped around the door handle. I thought about waiting until we hit a red light and jumping. That would be better than being in the mothermobile with him and his lessons about taste and age.

"Look, you can order whatever you like, okay?"

"Maybe this wasn't such a good idea anyway. Maybe I should go home and be with GG."

He stopped the car. Looked my way. "I think this is exactly what your grandmother wants for us tonight. Can't we make the best of it? Is it really that hard for you to be here with me?"

I could smell the cologne on his skin and it bothered me that he was wearing it at all, and then it bothered me because it smelled like the same one Johnny had in his bathroom on top of the toilet tank. "Do you really want me to answer that?"

Mark turned the dial on his car radio and punched the first button until some strange plinky-plunky music drifted out of the speakers. I listened for a minute, waiting for the words, but there were none. "I'm afraid it's this or Max's baby tunes. The radio doesn't play."

"What *is* this?" I asked.

"It's a tape from Annie's yoga & meditation class."

I nodded. All at once it seemed as if Mrs. Anne Darrow Madrid, totally together businesswoman, was hiding her messy, meditating mother side. I'm not sure why, but in that moment I liked her a little bit more. Maybe it was because my own mom liked to do yoga. A flash went off in my brain, Mom and Anne Madrid side by side doing a downward facing dog. Mark didn't say much for the next five minutes until he flipped the radio off. "It *is* pretty awful, huh?"

I nodded again.

"Well, at least we found one thing we can agree on."

"There's that," I said, "and I'll bet there's even one more."

"Yeah?"

"Yeah. I think we can both agree that you have a lot to learn about being a father."

Mark scratched the side of his head. "All right. I agree. But I'm trying to learn. It may not be something you believe, however I am trying."

"Why? For Max? For GG? For Anne?"

"No, Chessie. For you."

Mark didn't end up ordering a duck of any color. I said I wanted spaghetti and meatballs, and he said that sounded good and ordered the same. I wound mine up into a huge funnel on the end of my fork, while Mark twirled once and used both a fork and a spoon together to eat it. I gave him a curious crooked eyebrow look, which he dismissed.

"Chessie, Annie and I have settled into a nice house just minutes outside of St. Louis. There are plenty of bedrooms and we hope you'd consider staying with us for a while. It would make the trips to see your new doctor a whole lot easier." He said it in only one breath.

"I know all about your house and your bedrooms. I'm going to have to think it over." I shoveled a slice of Italian bread smothered in olive oil and tomatoes into my mouth.

He swallowed a swig of ginger ale. "I think it might be a good thing."

"You're pushing."

"I'm sorry. I really want us to spend some time together."

"All of a sudden? Because you think there might not be much time left? Well don't sweat it, Mark. There's a good chance I'll beat this thing and then you can disappear again."

Mark reached across the table and touched my hand. "No, Chessie, that isn't it."

I burned his fingers with my laser beam glare. "You're kidding me," I snarled, referring to his hand, which he promptly removed.

I'd scared away the conversation, scared it all away. We were in a silence so tight it strangled even me.

"Your kid is cute," I said quietly, in case my mother was watching and waiting for me to be polite.

"Thank you. He's your half-brother, you know."

"I can do the math."

"Max reminds me of you, when you were that age. Same nose, same pudgy chin."

"Excuse me? My chin is not pudgy."

Mark reclined in his chair and ran two fingers across his eyebrow. "Not now. I meant when you were a baby."

"I don't believe you can remember back that far."

"I have pictures."

"Good for you." I started for my glass and missed, tipping it over instead. Water rushed into his plate. Mark jumped up, lifted the cloth napkin off his lap and sopped up the spill.

"Sorry," I mumbled.

"No problem," he muttered, then waited for a busboy to refill my glass before he spoke again. "Chessie, this isn't only something your grandmother wants. In fact I want this more than I can probably ever convey."

I sipped and swallowed, sat up and dug my nails into the sides of my thighs. "Be careful what you wish for, Mark. Sometimes it actually comes true."

## Revelations

Meg was planning to sleep over. She was going to come by as soon as Mark brought me home.

"You'll need to vent," she'd said. "Do you think Sara could come too?"

"*No*. I mean, I don't even know her that well," I'd answered earlier in the evening.

"Fine, whatever. I'll be there by 9:30."

My date with Mark was finished by nine. I came in the house to find GG in the center of the sofa looking small and lost and hopeful. I'd run out of brat steam and besides she really didn't deserve it.

"How did it go, Chessie?"

I raised my eyebrows and nodded my head. "Not bad."

She was in her red gingham housecoat. It matched the table-cloth at the restaurant. Her eyes flashed a tiny white spark. "Do you want to talk about anything?"

"Maybe another time. Meg will be here real soon. She's spending the night."

"That's fine, dear. Would you like me to bake some brownies for you girls?"

"GG we're not twelve!" I gave her my first official easy smile of the night.

Hers was brighter than I'd seen in a while. "Then I'll turn in and leave you two to your fun."

I climbed the steps to my room, making it halfway up before

the gripping pain started in my ribs. I was on the top landing when the spasm began spreading like a band around my waist.

I willed it away, even though that had never worked before. I let my hair down and changed into my sweat shorts and a plain white tee. The whole time my chest was burning, my heartbeat erratic. It was stifling between my walls and I made a labored stretch for my air conditioner, flipping it on and embracing the rush of stale air. I fought the sense of suffocation until it demanded my undivided attention.

I descended the stairs, taking my time, running my hand along the tiny bumps in the wall. GG had already shut herself away in her bedroom so I opened the front door as softly as I could. Outside I searched the sky for a cluster of stars, not to wish on, to be sure I could still see. But the sky above was a dark, thick, heaven-less sheet of black. My fingers went cold, my toes went numb. The back of my neck was damp and prickly. My palms were wet.

Within seconds Meg's car raced toward the house. I raised my hand out to her. That was when it happened. I wasn't sure if I lost my footing. I went down, toppling over like a house of cards in a wind storm. I didn't remember much after that. Things went from hazy and dark gray to non-existent. I heard nothing, saw nothing. I wasn't aware of the terrible commotion I was told ensued. They said no matter what, they couldn't wake me, that I'd gone missing right before their eyes and stayed gone for nearly an hour.

The next thing I was sure of was the feeling of my bed, with its lumpy spots and wiry springs beneath me. I raised my lids and looked around again, at the blurry faces hovering in the air; GG, Doc Abner, and Meg, and two people I didn't recognize at first until I realized it was Mrs. Delafield and Mark Madrid. That's when it was confirmed to me that things were really as awful as I feared. Reality had bitten and I could not bite back.

"She's awake," Mark announced.

"Chessie? Chess, are you all right?" Meg asked.

"Move away, please give her some air," Doc Abner ordered.

"Chessie, can you hear me?"

I nodded. I could hear them all. I wanted to say something, but there was a huge wad of dry paper stuffed in my mouth.

Meg appeared stunned, like she'd survived an electric shock. Though it was my grandmother whose look immediately disturbed me. The cold cream on her face had track marks running through it from the tears she'd been crying. She was clutching a fistful of tissues, all damp and matted between her fingers.

Doc Abner dropped his cold stethoscope onto my chest and fixed a serious stare as he placed the opposite ends into his ears. For the first time since I'd known him, his hair was perfectly straight. He made a shushing sound to the small crowd who had been whispering stuff in front of me behind my back. The wheels were in motion. In the time it took for me to faint and awaken, I'd become the girl I never wanted to be, the girl everyone felt sorry for.

"Can you tell me what happened?" Doc Abner asked. Suddenly the room fell silent. I went to answer and realized that the huge wad of paper was my tongue.

I managed an "I need water."

"Water! She needs water. For God's sake get her some water!" Mrs. Delafield spat out and Meg and Mark both darted, but Meg shot him a warning look, and Mark held still.

Doc Abner lifted my eyelids and shined a teeny flashlight into my pupils. Then he felt my wrist for a pulse. "Have you eaten anything today?"

This time it was Mark that spoke. "She had spaghetti and meatballs. With me."

Meg hurried past him, leaving a suspicious gape in her wake. Maybe she thought he'd poisoned me. Maybe he had. "Here, Chess. Here's your water."

Doc Abner helped me sit up, and I drank first before I said a word.

"Can you tell me what happened, Chessie?" Doc Abner repeated.

"Yes," I said my voice barely above a whisper. "The fortune cookies lied."

★

Two days, three x-rays and four blood tests later, Meg and I sat in my backyard, under a heated sky that was melting away the final days of August. We were still friends, though I wasn't sure why. With my giant Big S secret uncovered, Meg should've been furious with me, ballistic, in fact, that I had never thought to trust her with it. She wanted to be. Yet if I were to die, how would it be if the last months we had together were spent in anger? It pissed me off, kind of. I mean, it was not authentic Meg. It was that damn pity working against me. She was hurt though, wore it like a huge H across her chest.

"If I'd have known you had this problem, I could have helped you all along," she said, still harping on it, days later.

"How exactly?"

The blue was beginning to grow out of her hair at the roots. She had a blotchy sunburn across her shoulders. "I don't know, Chess, maybe by being a friend for you, a pair of ears, somebody to listen, to lean on."

"But that's not how it is between us. You've always been the one with the issues, some guy trouble or something and I've always been the one to help you. I didn't want things to change. I didn't want them to be different." With a firm squeeze, I forced the last dollop of lotion from the bottom of the bottle and frosted my ankles.

"But they are," she replied. No shit. Meg would never be so patient with her disappointment. She was a rant and raver, which used to make me laugh, which would proceed to set her off even more until she wound up laughing at herself.

"I'm sorry I didn't tell you sooner."

"Sooner? Chess, you've had this disease for like two years or something! Jeez."

"Sorry."

Meg blew a sigh, stood up and paced a controlled line

between the lawn and the concrete walkway.

I looked up. "Who else knows now? Do your parents know? Does Johnny know?"

"Chess, its Eden's Pond. Everybody knows."

I nodded and bit the lower left corner of my lip.

"So are you going to go to Mark's for a while?"

I shrugged my right shoulder. "I guess so. GG's begging me to. She said she'll come too, in time to spend Thanksgiving and Christmas."

Meg plunked down into the grass that was dry, tan and overgrown. "So this Doctor Bird…is he like the best guy for stuff like this?"

"It's Doctor Pigeon."

"Oh, right."

I shook my head. "Doctor Bird."

"Whatever."

I gave her a shove and she toppled over. She managed a forgetful grin. I tossed a pebble at her and she tossed one back, even though deep inside surely she wanted to drop a boulder on my head.

✵

*It's Eden's Pond. Everybody knows.* I walked into the Dairy Maid on Thursday night just after my boss was gone for the day. I had called him earlier to say I was quitting. He didn't even ask why, just wished me well. I went in to find George. He was filling the cup dispenser and avoiding my face.

"Hi, George."

"Hello, Chessie."

I leaned into the countertop, my hands under my chin. "I wanted to say goodbye."

He still didn't make eye contact. "Oh?"

"Yeah, I quit today. I have to go to St. Louis and stay with my father, so…"

"I'm quitting too." George straightened his name tag. It said, "Gorge."

"Why? You're so good at this."

He shook his head. "Nah, this place sucks. Besides I'll be starting school in less than a week. Community college, for now. After two years I'll probably transfer away."

"Well, anyhow…it was good working with you. No matter what you do, you're going to be a huge success. I know it." I began to go.

"Chessie."

I turned.

At last he met my gaze. "You still owe me a dinner. So, when you come back from St. Louis, we should go. It would be the decent thing to do."

He didn't say *if* I came back. He said *when*. Yet it was Eden's Pond. Everybody knew I was sick. Even George.

I swallowed my extra saliva. "Well I did promise to be decent."

I was nearly to my car when he bolted out the double glass doors. "Chessie!"

"Yeah?"

"Hurry home."

# Humble Pie

Wilma at the dry cleaners survived a pleurisy that by rights should have killed her decades ago. Our mailman Fred's first cousin is a marathon runner from Illinois with only one lung. Mrs. Delafield's brother-in-law was born with a total of twelve fingers, six on each hand and supposedly he's a heart surgeon now. In a little less than a week Eden's Pond had become a three-ring circus and I was their latest bearded lady. GG said the tales were meant to inspire me, the whole "miracles can happen" mantra. Even Logan was chanting, all the way from Louisiana saying how her roommate at Tulane was in remission from leukemia for four years and counting. It might have been kind yet I had the feeling it was more like everyone was secretly glad they weren't me.

One odd exception was Anne Darrow Madrid. She called every other day to see how I was doing. She talked to me like I was a regular person and not like Mark's formerly abandoned daughter, the kid with the black cloud hung over her. I had a feeling she was the type of mother my own mom would have been friends with if she could. I wanted to ask her, every other day, why she was with *him*. What made her so sure she wasn't his next victim? Yet for some reason she was becoming somebody I didn't want to hurt.

GG was helping me pack my things. Part of me wanted her to come along, too, right away. But she thought it best that I had some time alone with Mark before she arrived.

"Why is that again?" I asked her. We were side by side on my bed, folding shirts into tight squares. Hers were much neater than mine. I tried to mimic the way she tucked each sleeve back evenly.

"Chessie, if I go immediately it'll be so easy for it to be you and me with Mark on the side. There would be no adjusting, no coming together for the two of you. I want to give you a chance to get acquainted with him. I'd just be a distraction."

"That's absurd," I said although I was sure it was completely true.

"Are you certain you don't want Mark to come and pick you up and drive you there in his car?" My grandmother was wearing her pearl necklace. I found an old photo of her once, where she was wearing those same pearls and a strapless dress, all satin and shiny. Back then she wore dark red lipstick. Her mouth was the color of shrimp now and puckered into tiny rows like one too.

"I'm certain. I want to have my car with me." I sounded strong and official. Yet I glanced at my reflection in the mirror above my vanity. I was trailing luggage beneath my eyes, two large grey duffel bags. There was an ugly sore at the intersection of my top and bottom lip. My hair was greasy and totally without style, dangling there in a collection of limp noodles. And there were some bruises at my shins that were an unattractive shade of greenish-blue.

"What if you have an episode while you're driving? What if, God forbid, you faint again?"

I stared at the girl in the mirror pretending to be me. "Then I do." Sometimes there were no quick fixes, no way to reassure, no "don't worries" for the taking.

GG rolled six pair of socks into a tight ball.

"It's less than two hours away," I sighed. "Not two days. I'll be fine. I'll call you the second I get there."

I wasn't looking when I heard my grandmother sniffle. Then all at once she pulled the tissue from under her watchband and blew her nose. "I made a pie for you to take with you."

"Apple?"

"Rhubarb."

"That's my favorite."

She held my hand in hers. "I know."

★

On the morning of my scheduled departure, Johnny Lauten called to offer me a sympathy screw. I told him that in as much as I appreciated the kind gesture, it might be better off if he just screwed himself instead. Then Meg called to ask if I planned to drop by and say goodbye. So I drove the Shadow over to her place and pulled into her driveway, where she was waiting in a pair of white overalls, her thumbs hung in the front flap. I got out to join her. A September wind blew through the sleeves of my nylon jacket sending a shiver up my arms.

"Say, listen Chess…did my idiot brother do something stupid to you? I mean, it kind of feels like you two hate each other."

I was thinking I could leave Eden's Pond without her ever knowing about Johnny and me. But then I thought, she's my very best friend, and I'd lied to her for so long about the Big S. And she was biting mad yet I'd removed her teeth. She could hardly even muster a growl. It annoyed me too that she told her family and probably everyone else she could that I was sick. She said she didn't, though my gut said she did. She probably even told Sara. I turned my body into the breeze.

"I was seeing him," I blurted out.

"You were seeing who?"

"I was seeing Johnny."

It took her a moment to register what I said and then her eyes widened, got narrow and widened again. "What do you mean? Were *you* the girl he was hooking up with behind Sara's back?"

"For a little while, I guess. I wanted to tell you all along but I knew you would never understand—"

She backed away from the car. "No way. Shit. What's wrong with you? You helped him cheat on another girl? That isn't *you*, Chessie!" She was suddenly allowed to be angry. I gave her something to attach her emotions to. It was a parting gift, a consolation prize.

"I'm sorry. I didn't mean to lie. I just knew you would be upset."

"Why him? Why my freakin' brother?"

"Meg, the truth is I've liked him for as long as I can remember."

"Oh jeez!"

She was shaking her head, her feet pounding the cracked tar driveway. Barbed wire words spun off her lips. She lectured me about how friends don't keep secrets and friends don't sleep with each other's brothers and that, of all people, I should know better. Suddenly she was the moral equivalent of Mother Theresa, and I was some trashy street walking, two-bit hooker. She didn't really end her speech, so when she came up for air I saw that as my opportunity to make my getaway.

"Look, it's all over now. It's in the past. I have to get going, Meg. I'll call you when I get there, if that's okay."

Although she wasn't finished with her verbal beating, she sensed I was.

"Yeah, yeah, okay, I guess," she told me. Our goodbye hug was one sided, mine not hers.

☆

Honesty had a brand new scent. It was pipe tobacco laced with rhubarb. I was thinking that Mr. Delafield meant to keep me company as I drove. I was thinking maybe he wanted some pie. The radio was being scratchy and fickle so it was hard to drown out the echoes of the truth. For these past few years I'd all but ignored them. The Big S was just a catch phrase and not a formidable sparring partner. *Not true.* It was real and fully prepared to take me down, hard. My mother paid me ghostly visits from the great beyond. *Not true.* I had been merely dreaming her. She was positively gone. Johnny Lauten loved me enough to make all the lies worthwhile. *Not true.* He never even liked me enough to go that far. The wish list actually made all these things happen. *Not true.* The list was a bunch of sentences that equaled nothing more than a coincidence.

I followed Anne's directions, even stopping after an hour to pee. "The restrooms at the junction of I-44 and US 63 seem the most sanitary," Anne wrote, as a footnote highlighted in yellow, which I suppose was to underscore the reason for the stop. I took note of the condition of the stalls and the toilet bowls, which weren't disgusting, and I felt grateful for the tip. Another hour passed quickly, and I was off the highway looking for street signs and landmarks. I was exactly where I should have been, bringing me to a tree-lined stretch of neighborhood where all the houses had two car garages and the same color shutters and doors. It looked as if somebody had built one real nice one, made a hundred photocopies and lined them up right next to each other. They were twice the size of the house I grew up in and much newer. Not one had a front porch or a picket fence or a rusty mailbox on a post out by the roadway. I'd entered a cookie-cutter gingerbread universe, and although I was still in Missouri, it didn't feel like it to me anymore.

As I slowed my approach, the family Madrid stood gathered in the front door frame arranged like a Christmas card photo. Anne was waving wildly, and Mark's hand was up in a steady pose.

"Park in the driveway, Chessie!" Anne called out and I did, right beside the mothermobile. There was a small slate lawn sign tucked in between two neatly trimmed hedges. It said, "The Madrids" in black, Old English lettering. I wondered if this sign has traveled the world with the trio, adorning the landscape in all of the dumb places my father had called home.

"Welcome!" Anne said, her arms reaching me with a friendly hug, which I decided to allow. Mark took a back seat, his actions far less spontaneous. His way was to judge them first, take too long and then do nothing until the moment passed.

"How'd it go? Did you have any trouble?" he asked, taking my bag off the seat.

"No, none at all." Baby Max was attached to Anne's hip, his chubby legs wrapped tightly around her thin, sturdy bones. In one tiny fist he clutched a plastic rattle that he was trying to eat. He was a little cute, in that pale pink baby kind of way. It dawned on me that he was my brother, in the same half-baked scenario that made Logan my sister. GG had said there was a resemblance. I stared into his perfectly round face to try and find it. He grinned at me, showing off a pair of teeth, like two mini-Chicklets sitting in the bottom of his cherry red gums. As I passed him, he shoved his torso toward me, reaching out as though we were long lost friends.

"Oh look, Mark. He wants Chessie!" Anne was so excited she nearly bubbled over. "Chessie, Max wants you. Isn't that great? Here, take him."

In the blink of an eye he was in my arms for the very first time. His wispy hair smelled all powdery and I took an extra whiff without even thinking. My mother said that being a mom is something that comes natural to most women. As Max rested his cheek on my shoulder, I had a sudden flash of panic that insisted I may never know that for myself.

"I'm tired." I handed him to Anne.

Mark checked me over with his worried dad eyes. "I'm glad you're here," he whispered. "Come on, I'll show you to your room."

I didn't want to remind him that my room was in Eden's Pond. I didn't want to start so soon. My head was heavy and my tongue felt twice its normal size. The next episode had waited long enough. In honor of my new baby brother I decided to take things slow—baby steps and all.

# Baby Steps

She'd decorated my room in shades of purple and blue, although Anne referred to them as violet and sapphire. I tried for a few minutes to recognize the difference, but I couldn't. Anne thought they were calming colors, "conducive to a good night's rest." It was the biggest room on the second floor, easily three times the size of the one I had slept in my whole life, and the only one of four that was completely decorated. "I hope you like it, Chessie. I asked the girl who babysits for Max what type of things eighteen year-olds prefer to have in their bedrooms these days."

Apparently they preferred to have lots of mirrors and a closet you can fit a small car in. It seemed they favored dream catchers at the sides of the windowsills and white silky curtains that looked like scarves rich women wore when it wasn't cold outside. There was a television on top of a table meant to hold it and bookshelves built right into the wall.

"I remembered you said you have lots of books," Anne explained happily. I had packed exactly two paperbacks, hardly shelf worthy at all. We toured the entire house, which Anne had dressed up in some sort of Country French style. I knew that because she said it over and over. I didn't think GG's house had a particular style, and we'd managed all right for the most part. Max's nursery was on the first floor, right outside of Mark and Anne's bedroom. His room had a theme too—monkeys. There were baby monkeys and grown-up monkeys, brown ones, black ones, orange ones and a couple of monkeys with polka dots. I thought it was an odd choice for a baby's room until Anne explained.

"When I discovered I was pregnant with Max, your father began having these conversations with my stomach. They'd always begin like this, 'Hey there, little monkey!' And then when Max was born it became a nickname that stuck." When Anne spoke she had this electric current that ran through her voice. I wasn't sure if she was always nervous or always "on" like a 60 watt bulb with no off switch.

"That's cute," I said for the sake of her light bulb. "It looks like you've been living here for a very long time."

"I know. I have this compulsive need to make a quick home wherever I go. I hang pictures before I fill the fridge."

Maybe Anne was justified. Maybe building a life with Mark Madrid and his collection of addresses meant being part nomad part homemaker and never being quite sure how long either would last. Two hours later she was gone to some appointment she said she couldn't break, and I retreated to the purple room where for the first time I noticed the ceiling had a skylight. I was busy staring up when I heard the knocking.

"Yes?"

"Chessie? May I come in?" It was him, *already* invading my space.

"Fine." I kept my eyes fixed above as he entered.

"Is something wrong?" he asked.

"What's with the window on the roof?"

Mark smiled. "It's a skylight. They're common to the newer built homes. Haven't you ever seen one before?"

Did he really think I was *that* stupid? "Not in person. Is there a shade for it?" The Big S had left me feeling cranky and a little mean.

"No, there isn't supposed to be."

"What happens if the people flying by in airplanes look in when I'm changing?"

He smiled again. I didn't. "That's not possible. I think you'll come to enjoy it actually."

"I doubt it. I prefer my privacy and my ceilings without holes in them."

Mark sighed. It was preposterous, and I knew it as well as he did. But my coming here wasn't his ticket to automatic forgiveness. He would have to earn it, and I was going to make sure he did eighteen years worth. "Look, I wanted to tell you to feel free to help yourself to anything you need. The kitchen is at your disposal."

"Anne already told me, and she showed me where all the food and stuff is."

"Okay, good. Later on, if you like, we'll show you around town."

"Maybe. I don't know. I'm kind of shot."

"I'm sorry. I just want to say how sorry I am that you're going through this." He stood there with his hands dangling at his sides like a big, unsteady ape.

"Don't be. Not for that. If you're going to be sorry, be sorry for being a lousy father. Be sorry for what you did to my mother. Be sorry for what you did to Logan and her mom." To hell with baby steps. I sat, hoping it would serve as his cue to leave. It didn't. Instead he blew out his breath and sat too, on the floor, and leaned against the closet door.

"Look, I know you have no reason to forgive me. I know I've been nothing other than a major disappointment for you as fathers go. And you can punish me if you want to. But you're here, and I'm here and, I think we could both make better use of the time."

"I wasn't planning to punish you," I said, though I was lying.

"Chess, I want to believe this could be the start of a whole new direction. Anne said Doctor Pigeon is highly respected in his field. We need to get you better first."

I tinkered with the heel of my tennis shoe. I had half a mind to slip it off and fling it at him. *We* need to get you better. *We.* Our little therapy session had been called on account of his giant balls. I stood up.

"I have some phone calls to make."

"Okay, no problem." He climbed to his feet. "There's a cordless phone in the hallway. I'll be out in the yard if you..."

"Sure, right, thanks," I said, ushering him out the door. It wasn't until he was down the stairs that I allowed myself to breathe deeply again. I grabbed the telephone and locked the door.

★

"I miss you already, GG. I don't think it's going to work, my being here with him." I was cradling the receiver between my chin and shoulder.

"You've only been there for an hour. Please, sweetheart, give it some time. Do it for me. Do it for your mom."

"When are you coming?"

"Soon. Let's see what the doctor has to say. Anne said you have an appointment tomorrow."

"I guess so."

"We'll speak right afterward."

"I guess so." I was being ten, maybe eleven.

"I miss you already, too. And I'm not the only one. A young man was by here earlier to see you."

A young man? Johnny? George?

"Really, who?"

"That Harris boy."

I fell back into the mattress. "GG, Cole Harris is not a young man. He's a lunatic. What did he say? What did he want?"

"He said he wanted to see how you were doing."

"I'll bet. Look if he shows up again, don't tell him one single thing. Not one, okay?"

"Of course, dear. Don't worry. People want to show their concern, that's all."

I told her I loved her before I hung up the line. She saw the good in people even when it didn't exist. I was relieved all at once to be in a place where I was practically unknown. I could walk down the street and not have a nosy neighbor greet me with a whisper and a wave. I was happy to be someplace where there was no Cole Harris and no Johnny Lauten, for that matter. The only boy I wanted to have anything to do with now wore Pampers.

✭

When Anne finally got home we had an early dinner, a large pepperoni pizza and a side salad with weird looking vegetables on top. I could hear GG's voice inside my head. She was remarking on how nobody bothered to prepare a home cooked meal on my first night in St. Louis and what a terrible shame that was since you couldn't undo something that wasn't done right once it was all over with.

Anne brought up taking me out to tour the town again, and I said yes to her only because I had said no to Mark and I thought it might annoy him. If it did, he refused to let on. In fact, my little plan to make Mark feel badly failed big time. He practically skipped out to the car and took the wheel as if he was a four-year-old heading to the candy store with a pocket full of quarters. Anne deferred the front seat to me, saying she needed to sit in back with Max. This news made Mark grin even wider than before. I was ready to bolt at a moment's notice if he felt the need, in his excitement, to touch me again.

Nothing about their town was all that impressive, and the driving only made me miss the familiar roads of Eden's Pond. As Anne chatted on from behind me about the mall and the places she saw teenaged boys gathering, I sought out the likes of a Dairy Maid or a bowling alley or a lake beside an open field of daisies.

As night fell on my first day in the Madrid household, I arranged my pillows and blankets on the floor, directly in line with the skylight above. I told myself that my mom had seen fit to punch that giant hole right through the roof tiles and rafters so she could keep a watchful eye on me. My sleep came easier that way.

## Preserves

The walls of Doctor Pigeon's office were covered in certificates in wood frames and plastic frames and acrylic frames all announcing without a shadow of a doubt that he was not pretending to be a doctor. The glass jars on his countertop were filled with cotton swabs and bandages, precisely prepared and careful not to be smudged or empty. While Anne fell into a deep brown leather couch in the waiting area, a crisp, dainty nurse with squeaky shoes led me to the exam room. It had been pre-determined that Mark not be the one to accompany me on these visits, so he was at home having to be a hands-on dad to baby Max, like it or not.

I was perched on the edge of the table, conscious of the curve in my spine and straightening up several times, until ultimately hunched again. Within minutes he knocked and entered, looking very much the professional MD, all white coat, navy blue slacks and a Cardinals baseball cap on top of his head. Huh?

"Chessie? I'm glad you're here." He spoke to me through paper thin lips, almost as if the top and bottom were both the same.

"Thank you."

The formalities of my appointment didn't take very long. He was a grunter. Throughout my vitals, grunt. He summoned another nurse by way of pressing a button on the telephone. They didn't converse. He grunted. She nodded to comply. It wasn't a nasty grunt or even one that showed disinterest, simply a busy, technicalities-at-hand grunt. And speaking of hands, his were small and his nails were coated in a clear shiny coat of polish. It sent a jolt through my body. Meg always said if God wanted guys to get manicures he wouldn't have stuck hair on their knuckles. She may have been right. This was supposed to be the man who, for all intents and purposes was going to help save my life? I'd wanted him to be burly and tough like a cowboy with a holster and a ten-gallon hat. Yet he was almost petite and wearing a baseball cap, of all dumb things.

He made very little small talk with me. The usual how have you been feeling relay to which I replied, "Like a storm is brewing inside me."

"There is," he said, without apology.

I expected the sad look to follow, the one Doc Abner used to offer. It didn't come.

"Chessie, I'm not a fan of the latest x-ray results. When I see something I don't like I have to do what I can to change it. If that means we get aggressive, then we do. We're on the same page here. Our goal is united."

"Okay."

He wrote in his doctor diary, a long, quiet entry. All at once I missed Doc Abner and his bad wig.

"Doctor Pigeon?"

He looked up. "Yes?"

"I used to ask my other doctor how long he thought I had to live, mostly because on some level, maybe on all levels, I didn't really believe him. I want to ask you the same question. Yet I'm afraid of what you might say."

"I'm not ready to commit an answer to that one." He clicked his pen and returned it to his pocket.

"Fair enough."

He handed me two sheets from his prescription pad. "Take your medicine. I'll see you in a week."

And all at once, our visit was over. For a second I imagined I'd leave to find GG sitting with Mrs. Abner talking the business of strawberry preserves. But it was Anne rising to meet me with a satisfied smile.

"How did it go?" she asked.

"I have homework," I told her, presenting the two papers, the recipe for my own preservation.

✶

Back at the house, Mark had made tuna salad sandwiches for lunch. He played with the baby and tried desperately to catch my eye. Shortly after we ate, Anne announced that the air outside smelled like autumn and she was going to take Max for a walk and did I want to come?

I said I did and met her out on the front doorstep. The baby had a steady line of spit that ran from his mouth to his chest, and Anne swooped down to try and catch it every chance she could. It was she and I and the Monkey, and I was grateful Mark had something else to do. We strolled along, her mouth keeping time with our feet. I had to wonder how a woman like that ever ended up married to a man like him. It wasn't long before she volunteered the answer.

"I met your father at work. I was a social worker and he came in for treatment."

She was wearing a burgundy sweater that went all the way down past her knees and clogs that made a light clunking sound as she stepped.

I stared at her until she went on.

"I did his intake. We had only two meetings and then I assigned him another therapist."

"Why?"

"Because, I realized I had the potential to have feelings for him that I shouldn't have. So I thought it best that he be seen by another counselor. Yet every time he came in for his appointments with her he smiled at me and said hello, and every time, it confirmed that the attraction was mutual."

"Why was he there to begin with?" I didn't know if I was asking her to breach some doctor/patient privilege, and I didn't care.

"Well, he was trying to work on some personal issues. He wanted to understand himself and why he made the choices he did. I saw his pain. I felt for him. He was ready to fix whatever he had to in order to make things right in his life."

I pulled my denim jacket in close to my body. "Did he?"

"He came consistently. Even though he wasn't my patient, I followed his progress the best I could. My reasons were selfish, I suppose. Eventually, I invited him to dinner, and we began to see one another outside of work, once a week and then more frequently."

"And you fell in love and got married?"

Baby Max let out a loud cry, alerting his mother that he'd dropped his bottle, and he wanted it back.

Anne stopped the carriage, and I lifted the bottle off the ground for her.

"No. Not quite," she said, taking it from me. "I fell in love, and then I got pregnant." Gone was the electricity in her voice. A stoic hush took its place. "It was a surprise, really. You see, I was once told I'd never have a child. So this little boy is my miracle."

I looked down at the child Mark called Monkey and Anne called a miracle. I knew right then that there were two sides to every story and two stories to every child, including me.

✪

Later that day I closed myself in the room they referred to as mine with the telephone in my hand once again. I placed two calls. The first was to Meg but I spoke to Mr. and Mrs. Lauten, one after the other, who each said, "No, Meg's not home." If there was some plan underway for Meg to ignore me then I'd say the wheels were in motion. I'm wasn't sure if my eleventh-hour confession sealed the fate of our friendship. If so, it may not have been worth the purge. I wanted to tell her about Doctor Bird and his manicure. I knew she would laugh about it and then make me laugh, too.

I hung up and dialed again.

"God, Chessie, I can't believe you're actually there!" Logan gushed, acting impressed because I was calling from Mark's house.

"I'm here."

"How is it? What's it like?"

I looked around. "It's big, kind of nice, I guess. There's a bunch of rooms up here that nobody's using. Anne said one is for you, if and when you decide to come."

"Wow. She seems pretty cool."

"Anne is very cool. If it weren't for her and Doctor Pigeon I wouldn't have made the trip."

"How is Mark?"

I shook my head. "Nervous. He needs a shave and maybe a haircut. And he can hardly stand me. I think one of us may kill the other any day now. Keep an eye on the news."

Logan chuckled. "I miss you, Chess."

"Me too, Logan. I wish you were here. Things would be balanced. Now it's like me against them, in a way, and only because she's linked to him."

"If Aunt Vicky isn't out of jail by the end of the month then maybe I'll come for Thanksgiving."

"Okay."

"Chess?"

"Yeah?"

"How are you?"

I wanted to answer the way Dr. Pigeon had. I'm not ready to commit an answer to that one, Logan. Instead I said, "I'm fine."

It's hard to break the habit of lying once you've done it for what feels like forever.

"It's great to hear your voice."

"You too, Logan."

No lies there, just nothing but the truth.

Afterward I reached into my suitcase, still more packed than unpacked, reached far into the inside pocket and pulled out the wish list, now folded in fours. I flattened out the creases with the side of my hand and studied the hopeful curves in my penmanship.

I silently asked my mom to come again and tell me if I'd wished correctly. It seemed I had and yet in my heart, I still couldn't tell.

## Wish #3

My grandfather, Alan Lowenstein the 1st, was an inventor. He had something to do with the creation of the shopping cart, I think, or it may have been the thing that holds the shopping carts. Whichever it was, it was the thing that brought him his riches and the thing that brought those same riches to my father. GG told me Mark's parents really didn't mean to leave any money to him, although he got it anyway on account of a technical glitch in the way the will was worded. So, my father, the carefree, rogue world traveler, who likened himself to a modern day Peter Pan, had the good fortune to have inherited his good fortune. And while he always paid for the stuff I needed while I was growing up, his money was a poor substitute for his presence.

I had come to see that Mark was living off whatever cash he had left, which surely had to start running out soon. It was Anne who had been the official breadwinner, at least right up until she gave birth to the baby she never imagined she'd have.

"He dabbles now," Anne told me, as she diapered Max.

"Dabbles?"

"Yes, he wants to start his own investment firm so he's doing his research. Your father has a great business mind. I believe he can make this happen." I think she was trying to say if it didn't happen, the well would run dry as the Sahara. "It's a good thing to have a plan for your future. Do you have one, Chessie?"

Max shot a line of pee directly toward the ceiling.

"To stay alive."

Anne stepped aside, covered her child and didn't flinch. "What about a career path?"

"I want to be a pilot. I want to fly planes."

She used her forearm to itch her nose, lifted Max off the changing table and then smiled. "I love that. You will fly planes. I can feel it. Anyway, your father is very, very happy you're here."

If he was really happy with two verys in front I think I would've been able to tell. Still, she seemed so convinced that I hated to debate her right then and there.

She continued, "He'll need to spend more time than he prefers to in preparation of this investment venture. However if it all comes together in the end it will have been worthwhile."

I couldn't see where she was going, not in that moment. However Anne Darrow Madrid was not a woman who said things for the sake of hearing herself talk. She had her reasons.

✯

"Where's Mark?" I asked. Anne and I were having dinner alone, for the third night in a row.

"He's at the library again." She made it sound completely rational. She had to.

"Research?"

"Yes," she replied. She kept her eyes on the vegetable lasagna she'd heated from out of the freezer. Baby Max was hanging out of his little chair sideways. A scent wafted through the air declaring that he'd filled his diapers. She didn't seem to notice.

"Anne, may I be excused?"

"Sure, Chessie."

When I left the house she didn't ask where I was heading. It was raining and dark and only six p.m. I had learned the way to the public library and went there once to see how it compared to the one in Edenville.

It was much larger than ours with rows and rows of brand new books and glossy wood desks. I parked my car and barged my way in until I remembered I needed to be quiet. I eyed each section suspiciously; hoping to find him there, his nose buried in a pile of books stacked two feet high. *Research, must do the research.* The first floor was loaded with people, none of whom were my father. I sprinted down the long stairway to the lower level and then spun quickly on my tiptoes through the rooms, scanning the faces of St. Louis's most studious. He was nowhere to be found. I turned to go, heading up the steps with my mind playing guessing games. It was when I reached the lobby and took one last look inside that I noticed the door to the men's room swing open. Mark came out and walked over to a table in the corner. I followed him and watched as he took a seat beside a woman in a bright blue sweater and brighter red lipstick. He touched her arm and said something to which she laughed. It was like watching Johnny and Sara at the bowling alley only I had no bat or ball to deflect my anger.

"What is this? What are you doing?" My voice was squeaky and high. I wanted to scream at him and shake him until his head tumbled off.

"Chessie." His face went blank.

"That's right," I said. I kept my focus straight ahead. If I looked at her I might just lose it.

"Let's talk," he said.

"Oh yes, let's." He rose to his feet and led the way.

I was saying things my grandmother wouldn't like, careful to keep them under my breath, if only to obey the library rules. I didn't care if *he* heard me. I was hoping he did. I trailed him out to the parking lot and stopped outside of his car, squaring my feet shoulder width apart, my hands firmly on my hips, my eyes staring him down. I was rock, paper and scissors. I was David to his Goliath. He spoke first. The tone in his voice said he wanted to scold me, or yell if he could.

"What do you think you're doing here?"

"I'd like to ask you the very same thing. Who is *she*, Mark? Why are you here with *her* and not at home with your wife and child?" I could feel the blood running up my neck and coating my skin in a thick blush.

"In the first place that woman is a business colleague and Anne knows all about her. Do you actually believe if I were doing something wrong I'd be so stupid as to do it in a place my wife knows I am?" He pushed his hair behind his ear, thinking he'd made a triumphant point. I begged to differ.

"*You* have no right to be here at all. You have a family, *another one* that's relying on you. You're going to do it again, aren't you? You're going to drop out of their lives like you did to me and my mom and Logan and her mom. Who the hell do you think you are?"

At first my finger was pointing at him with my wicked accusations that were ugly and true at the same time. And then, all at once, my arms left my control and lunged toward him, delivering a steady stream of shots fired at his chest. Before I knew it, I was beating away, hammering him with every ounce of strength and fury that I had kept carefully under wraps until then. He grabbed me by the wrists to restrain me.

"Chessie, Chessie, please stop. Calm down. There are people watching. Please calm down."

He held onto my hands until I doubled over, dissolving in tears that had been waiting for so long to arrive. He pulled me in to his chest where he placed my head. I laid there only long enough to catch my breath and speak.

"I had to come to St. Louis to face what's happening to me, to face who I really am. Don't you think it's time you did the same?"

Mark dropped to the ground, taking a seat on the curb beside his front tire.

He kept his chin down. I stood over him, Wish Number Three hanging in the weight of my words.

"You have no idea how much you hurt the people who want to love you. I hate what you did to my mother. Still, if I try really, really hard I might be able to understand. I don't know much about love between two random people who come together by chance, yet I know it can be messy and disappointing. But that doesn't explain what you did to *me*. I'm your daughter. When I bleed it's half your blood. We weren't supposed to be strangers. We were supposed to be a family, you and me. It may have been too hard to stay with my mother because your heart led you away, but you left me, too."

I didn't realize I was still crying. I tasted the bittersweet salt as the tears ran from my eyes and into my mouth. Mark held the top of his head, blocking it off as if he imagined I might hit him again. His shoulders heaved up and down and before long I heard his sobs, low, guttural, like a wounded animal.

"I know who I really am. I'm a screw-up. I'm a loser. Do you know how hard it is for me to like myself after all that's happened? After all I've done wrong in my life, after all the people's lives I've destroyed?"

I slowly folded to my knees. "Don't do it all over again."

He blinked and rubbed his palms across his eyes. "I'm not having an affair with that woman."

"Anne barely eats. She barely takes care of Max. She's worried about what's happening, Mark. You need to tell her all of this. If you leave it unsaid, she's going to assume the worst. It's all anybody knows of you." I wiped my face on my sleeve. In an instant he took hold of my arms and pulled me in.

"I've only now got you back. I don't want to lose you, ever, ever again."

I swallowed the pain in my throat. "I'm not sure if there's all that much I can do to change the outcome of my life, Mark, but I think you can change yours."

We sat in silence until his hug fell open and I slipped away. Above our heads two giant evergreens tipped and swayed in a breeze that stayed out of reach. Some people moved silently by concealing curious glances behind the clear plastic jackets of the books they'd checked out.

He got up first and then I did. "I really did love your mother, Chessie."

"She loved you more," I said.

He shook his head, "No. She was just better at it."

✭

I arrived home at Mark and Anne's to find a letter waiting, a letter from Meg.

I'd called her once more, since the first time when she had her folks say she wasn't there. That time it was their machine suggesting I leave a message at the tone. I chose not to.

*Dear Chess,*

*We've been best friends for years and you know me better than anyone else. So you'll know why I have to say how I feel. You were the sister I never had. When Logan came and you were so happy, it made me jealous because I guess I thought you and I were sisters, in a way. I guess I thought you felt the same way I did. I never kept one single secret from you. Not even one. But in these past few months I've found out you kept your whole life from me, your problems, your pain, your emotions, everything. I have no idea who you are anymore. It's like I've been betrayed.*

*I want to talk to you. Every day I want to call. Yet I can't. I know you know a thing or two about the process of forgiveness. I am in the process of trying to forgive the lies you told me, most of them by omission, some flat out.*

*GG tells me you are seeing the new doctor. Chess, I pray for you, that you will get well. And I love you. Always know that to be true.*

*Meg*

I read it three times before I put it inside the flap of my suitcase, the one where I kept the wish list. I had spent the early part of my night giving Mark his what-for. It made perfect sense that I spent what was left of the hours being given my own.

## Fluoride & Flats

I wanted to be a kid again. Not like a little child—a girl who wore makeup and cool clothes. A girl who got all dressed up to go out and meet other kids her same age. Anne told me about a club for teens where they didn't serve alcohol and there was a DJ and a place hang out. She took me to the mall and I bought a new outfit. I used to be a size 5. I had become a 3 quickly fading to a 1. I picked out a pair of dark blue jeans with a curly design on the back pockets and a pink silky sheer blouse with sleeves that hung down in a ruffle below my wrist. We got a pink camisole to put underneath. I kept thinking that Meg would have loved it.

The new medicine from Dr. Pigeon had been helping to keep the episodes away, but it gave me a rash behind my knees and on the underside of my elbows. It made me thirsty all the time so I always had to drink, which meant I then always had to pee. Still it was better than the way I'd felt when the Big S shook me up and then down. I dared to think I felt better. Going out was the next logical step.

"She can't go there alone."

Mark and Anne were in the living room watching Max who was crawling around in aimless circles. I was up in my room. Thanksgiving was less than a week away. GG was coming to stay until the end of the year. Logan's aunt had been released from prison in time for turkey dinner so she said she'd come the first week in December.

"She'll be fine, Mark."

"No. That's not a good part of town. Maybe, if we drive her and pick her up."

"Don't be silly. She's not a baby. She needs to feel independent now."

I felt bad eavesdropping yet I did it anyhow.

"It's out of the question, Anne."

"You're being stubborn—"

"No, you are."

They were arguing over me. I kept as still as I could and listened intently.

"Mark, please be reasonable. She's got to be bored stiff."

I heard the sound of what may have been his open hand hitting the coffee table.

"Dammit, Anne! I have to look out for her. We both do. That club is in a seedy area where all sorts of bad things happen. What if she were approached? She's in no shape to handle herself. Think about it, will you, please!"

Anne kept her voice low and steady. "I have thought about it and I want Chessie to feel like a young woman. I want her to have some fun."

"Find some other way. Either we drive her or she doesn't go."

I had wanted him to be a father. He thought it best to choose this as his first official fatherly act. I was angry and defiant. It took all my best efforts to refrain from marching down the stairs and telling him that he was not the boss of me, that he had no right to dictate my every move. Instead I scratched my rash and made a plan. Mark Madrid was not going to tell me what I could and couldn't do. Sure as hell, that wasn't happening.

✵

On Friday at 7:00 p.m. Anne and Mark and the baby were going to visit a friend of theirs. They'd asked me to come along. I faked a minor episode and they left me alone, leaving me with the phone number of where they'd be. "It's just around the corner," they assured me and I fingered the guilt in my mind pretending it had no justification.

"We'll be home no later than ten," Anne promised. She was dressed in a thick wool sweater and a pair of corduroy pants that made her trim frame look stocky.

"Call if you need anything at all," Mark said, checking me over with careful eyes.

I was wrapped in my terry cloth robe and a pair of fuzzy green socks. "I will."

It didn't take me long to change, although I took my time anyway. I put on two layers of mascara, one layer of blush and my brand new clothes, watching my reflection as if it was somebody else and not really me. I thought about the night I went to the lake with Johnny, how I snuck out and snuck right back in again. I'd had some practice with deceit.

At a little past nine I dashed off a note to Anne and Mark. It said I was restless and took a ride to get some air. I wrote that they shouldn't worry; I'd be home soon enough. At 9:30 I made my calculated escape, being certain first that their car was nowhere in sight.

In the Shadow, I thought about forgiveness, in theory. I figured there must be a point of no return where forgiveness is concerned. Or maybe the ability to forgive is a gene you either get or you don't. And I hadn't. Perhaps it's handed out to balance something else. Like good teeth. In eighteen years I'd had only one cavity. The dentist said I had fluoride in my blood. She has remarkable luck with her dental health, people would say as they referred to me, but not one ounce of capacity for mercy.

I tried to remember the way to the club. Anne had driven me by it on the day we went to the mall. I knew it wasn't too far from there. A few rights, a quick left. There'd been a Kwik-Stop on the corner, or was it a bank? I was slightly confused, cruising at a safe speed so I wouldn't miss anything. Before long I was like my little brother, crawling in aimless circles. I pulled into the parking lot of a small string of stores thinking maybe if one was open I could ask for directions. The motor shut down as I stepped outside, making a dash for the walkway. I scanned the row of tall glass windows and doors. Most all were dark except for a place that sold futons. I picked up my pace again and aimed for it. The showroom was black but I saw a light on in the back area. I banged on the metal frame around the windowpane. I waited a second or two and banged again. I squinted through the darkness to read a sign hanging on a door in the far corner of the store. It said "restroom."

"Excuse me? Hello?" I called out, cupping my mouth so that my voice might carry better.

Nothing.

I would need to find a gas station. Those places were always open. I walked away, with one final glance over my shoulder. As I got closer to the side of my car, I pulled out my keys and looked down. My front tire was spread out like black tar all over the pavement. "Dammit!" I said. I had never really learned how to change a flat or curse better. Now what?

The lot was oddly vacant, and it seemed as if I was the only person alive in St. Louis. I wanted to panic, though I forced myself to stay calm. I turned around to go. That's when I heard what sounded like a muffled cough and I swung my head to follow it. There, crouched on the ground just two cars from mine was what looked like a man, a big man, his body hunched over in a ball as if he were trying to be smaller and unseen. My breath stuck in my throat and my pulse tap-danced away. I forced my feet to flee, though they wanted to freeze or go limp and wobbly like Max's. I ran, all the while checking over my shoulder to be sure I wasn't being chased. Every door I came upon was closed up tight and suddenly the only two living souls in the world were me and the guy who was planning to kill me.

I heard footsteps or possibly my own heavy heartbeat, I wasn't sure which. I kept running until I spotted a phone booth. My hands were shaking so much I could barely dial. I prayed for them to be home. Then I prayed for *her* to answer.

"Hello?" Mark said.

"Mark, it's me. I need help!"

I blurted out where I thought I was and what was happening, twice because the first time he couldn't understand me. "Please hurry, please!"

"Chessie! Stay right where you are. I'm coming!" His voice was high and pitchy. It had taken me approximately eighteen minutes to get from Mark's to wherever I was then. It took him six. He flew out of the mothermobile as though his legs were wings, reaching me with a tight jaw and eyelids that were open extra wide like toothpicks were propped in there.

"Are you all right? Are you okay?" He grabbed me by the top of my arms.

"Yes, yes I'm just frightened."

"Where is he? Where's the man?" Though it was an especially cold, late November evening, Mark's face was covered in tiny beads of sweat. I pointed to where my injured automobile lay helpless and maimed.

"Get in," he ordered and we both climbed inside the minivan. He didn't say anything as we drove over to my car. I could see his chest heaving, his knuckles a tight reddish white against the brown leather steering wheel.

"Are you sure you're okay?" he asked again, his hand moving for the door handle.

"Yes."

I watched him search the immediate vicinity for any sign of my reported attacker.

But whoever the eerie stranger was and whatever he planned, would remain an unsolved mystery.

"I don't see anyone. He's gone, Chess. I'm going to change that tire for you. You have a spare in the trunk don't you?"

I nodded, and he sprang into action once again. My father, the infamous Mark Madrid had come to my rescue. And for the moment, for the very first time in a long, long time, I thought I might possibly be able to stand him.

I followed him home where we found Anne pacing the floors

with Max asleep in her arms. "Oh, thank God," she said as we came in. "Thank God you're all right."

They didn't yell at me or lecture me or even act like they were mad. I didn't offer the truth; that I was trying to find the club. And if they thought so, neither one said. Anne handed the baby to Mark then wrapped me up close to her chest, keeping me there for a minute. She had the scent of a mommy. I remembered it well. Then she excused herself to put the baby down.

Mark and I stayed in the living room where he sat back into the sofa and ran his fingers through his hair. He took a deep breath and slowly released it into the air.

"I'm sorry," I whispered.

"Look, Chessie…I'm only relieved nothing happened to you. It could have been a lot worse. That tire was definitely punctured. Who knows what that guy had in mind."

"Thanks, Mark. Thanks for coming."

Mark looked at me and smiled. "I'm going to get ready for bed. All this excitement's worn me out."

"Goodnight," I said.

"Goodnight, Chessie."

☆

Two hours later, I blinked up at the small part of the sky. Sleep was up there, miles away and not getting any closer. It wasn't all that late really, and I was thinking about my perfect teeth, my stubborn streak, my brush with death, and my best friend in the world. I tiptoed for the phone in the hallway.

"Meg? It's me."

"Chessie?" It was possible that I'd woken her up. "Is that you?"

"Yes. You were sleeping?"

"It's okay. How are you?"

"I'm all right. St. Louis is kind of a scary place. I got your letter."

There was a long pause where I thought she might have hung up, and then, "I miss you."

I heaved a sigh, two months in the making. "I miss you too. What's new?"

"I met someone. His name is Jack Wright. God, Chessie he's super cute. You can't even imagine. I mean, the stuff I want to do with him."

It was her way of saying that our storm was over. Meg had no issues with forgiveness, but she had a whole mouth full of shiny silver fillings. "Oh, before I forget, Shelly and I went to see that new Bruce Willis movie at the Multiplex last night, and that kid George from the Dairy Mud asked for you. He works there now. It's kind of cute, Chess, he's so obviously got the hots for you."

"That's crazy."

"*Oh,* and you won't believe who took George's old job…Cole Harris."

"No way!"

"Way."

Meg and I talked for one hour and forty-seven minutes. It turns out that everything and nothing had changed in Eden's Pond. I hung up feeling like the girl I had been for the majority of my life. I hung up forgetting that I'd almost been raped or mugged or worse, which was a good thing. I fell asleep seeing Mark Madrid in a race with some proposed evil stalker, his voice calling out to me, "Chessie! I'll save you!" And he had.

## For the Team

GG arrived by bus, on the day before we were supposed to give thanks for all that was right in our lives. I told the Madrids that I wanted to go by myself to pick her up and they saw no reason to insist otherwise. I'd practically forgotten how small she was, how ivory colored, how delicate and perfect. I ran to her, rushing her with all of me and nearly knocking her off her feet as I threw my arms around her neck. She'd never once held me that way, so tightly that I was sure she'd cracked my ribs.

"My sweet girl," she repeated again and again. And then she released me and set us apart. "Let me see you. Oh, you look wonderful."

"I feel good, GG. I do. I feel good."

I'd had a whole slew of visits with Dr. Pigeon and his white coat and Cardinals cap. Each time he gave me no indication of where I was, medically speaking. It was grunt, smile, grunt, needle, grunt, smile, pat on the knee. I didn't want to ask. For the first time in so many months, I didn't feel sick. What if the file in his hands with my name on it demanded he debate me?

Anne greeted my grandmother as if she'd known her forever. Mark was more cautious but GG was quick to put him at ease. If she ever hated him as much as I did, she'd found a way to let it go. Perhaps she was doing it for mom. I was equal parts surprised and impressed. The pieces of me were falling into place. The next morning brought the scent of rhubarb pie sweeping up the staircase to wake me. Anne made a turkey-less turkey since she was a vegetarian and nobody cared either way. She kept saying, "Save a bird, stuff an artichoke," which after a while wasn't all that clever. I kept care of baby Max, who was swiftly turning into one of my favorite people under two feet tall. I taught him to roll a ball into my open legs, which he did with a chubby tongued smile. During our supper Mark managed to find the relaxed side of himself—home field advantage I supposed. He was entirely different from the way he'd been at the barbeque dinner in Eden's Pond. We ate cornbread stuffing, pasta salad, string beans and Brussels sprouts smothered in melted cheese. I stuffed every inch of my gut until I needed to open the top button on my black denim jeans. It felt like the start of something big—a pilgrimage for the ages.

By day's end I met GG in the room Anne had designated to her, the one across the hall from mine. It was cloaked in a thick blue darkness with a small slice of moonlight splashed against the wall. She was dressed for bed in her long red flannel nightgown.

"What is it, darling?"

"I just wanted to see you once more."

And though her face was lost in the shadows, I knew she was wearing a weary smile.

★

December's dance was jazzy and slick. Anne could hardly wait to assemble a Christmas, mistletoe, tree and all even if it was still weeks away. I could hardly wait for Logan to arrive. I was craving a playmate, preferably one who was fully potty trained.

Logan arrived on a Friday, mid-morning, and we celebrated by having a "family" brunch at a restaurant in town, five blocks from where I'd nearly been killed. My sister's face was sullen and distracted, and I knew immediately she missed her mother more than she let on. It's something you can tell if you're in the motherless child club like we are. Anne was chatty and honestly oblivious to it all. She spewed on about whether cranberry sauce should come from a can or not.

After an hour the waitress brought the bill. Mark looked it

over while Anne took Max from the highchair near her. That's
when it happened. It was as clear as day and just as definite. The
little boy reached his two plump arms out toward his father and
said, "Da Da." It might not have been such a big deal, yet up until then he'd only ever said things like "ga ga" and "blumph"
and stuff that was on its way to becoming a real word but hadn't
made it there yet.

"He said Da Da!" Anne confirmed.

"I know!" Mark said. He wore a big, sloppy smile across his
lips. "That's right, Monkey. I'm Da Da. That's right! Come here."
He took the baby out of Anne's arms.

"Did you girls hear that?" Anne asked.

"Yeah," I said. GG clapped out loud.

"That's great," Logan agreed.

We shared a look among ourselves and a silent conversation. I
told her Mark had finally heard a child of his call him Dad again.
She told me she hoped he could make it last this time around.
Anne caught us in our unspoken commentary. Her eyes said they
wholeheartedly agreed with Logan.

★

It was five a.m. when I heard her rustling around from down
the hall. She was quiet and yet stirring enough to wake me. She
meant to.

"Chessie…are you up?" Logan stood in the doorway of my
room dressed in a large chenille blanket.

"Logan? What's wrong?"

She came in and sat in the middle of the carpet, her legs criss-
crossed in a tight bow, the blanket falling around her. She was
wearing thick, white corduroy socks that almost glowed in the
starlight streaming in from above. "I can't sleep."

"I had that too when I first got here. It's kind of like being
homesick for your own bed, right?"

"No. That isn't it."

"It's your mom, then? You're missing your mom."

She tipped her head up and down. "It's so hard at times like this. Christmas was her favorite holiday."

"My mom loved it too."

"Does it ever get easier, Chess? Does it get to a place where it doesn't hurt so bad?"

I sat down beside her, my legs assuming the very same position. "In a way, it does."

"I feel like I'm damaged or broken and unfixable. If I could have one wish, just one, it would be to see her again."

"It's the thing I want most of all," I said, my voice barely above a whisper.

She turned to me. She'd had her hair cut and it made her look older. "Chessie, what does the doctor have to say?"

"Not a hell of a lot. Although I'm feeling tons better. I have an appointment tomorrow. GG was going to come along. Do you want to come, too?"

"Yeah, I do. Chess?"

"Hmm?"

"Do you think it's going to work?"

"The medicine?"

"No, us and Mark being a family."

I stretched my neck back as far as it could go. I'd often look to the sky for guidance. I never did learn that it had precious little to offer. I checked my gut instead.

"It's a very good possibility."

We fell asleep there, the two of us, in heaven's view for the sake of those we'd lost who might still care to steal a glance.

✯

GG and Logan sat shoulder to shoulder in the low backed crayon colored chairs directly outside of Dr. Pigeon's exam room. The waiting area with its deep comfy couches was packed with guests. Business was good. As I left them to head in, GG thumbed through a Good Housekeeping while Logan fiddled with her new bangs.

"Hello," I said, taking him in. It was the first thing I noticed. His Cardinals cap was on backwards. A rally cap.

"Chessie, please sit down."

"No, thank you. It's bad news isn't it?"

"I had been hoping to see more."

"But, I haven't had an episode in so long. And I feel stronger."

"The meds are helping with the symptoms. They're managing the pain. Its progress I'm looking for and I hate to say, there hasn't been all that much."

"But there's some."

"Yes, some. So we move in harder. We hit it with all we've got."

"Okay. I can do that."

"I'll be switching things up. It might make things more difficult at first. Stay with me. Trust me."

"I will."

When I joined GG and Logan again they both stood up at once.

"Well?" GG asked.

"Its rally time," I said to Logan before I looked at my grandmother. "Say your prayers."

✮

We arrived home to find a tabletop of food waiting for us—Chinese food. I wasn't all that hungry anymore. GG and Logan did what they could to eat. Afterward Anne and my grandmother spoke quietly in the other room while Mark listened in.

"You can do this," Logan said, rubbing my forearm. "I have faith."

It was then that I began to lose what was left of mine. She reached for the fortune cookies, took one and left another in front of me. I stared it down, its brown toasted edges mocking my fear. I lifted it off the table, began to crack it and then set it down again. It was just a stupid biscuit and not a crystal ball. Those damn things were never right anyway.

## Holidazed

I referred to the weeks that followed as my shades of purple haze. First thing in the morning it was the mauve and magenta pills, chased by the violets at lunchtime. I took two plum-colored caplets with dinner and two puce at bedtime. Logan called them the purple people eaters since I'd been all but swallowed up whole by the sum of their actions. Time became irrelevant. Christmas was irrelevant. My thoughts were jumbled up and smashed into one another—incoherent, if I were lucky, nonsense, if not.

In the lucid moments I'd find GG staring out the windows with a face that had already assumed the very worst outcome. When they thought I wasn't able to decipher it, Anne and Mark would bicker in hushed tones over one silly thing or another while Max wailed over a new tooth he was cutting, and a brand new ear infection. At night, sleep either came rushing at me like a herd of crazed sheep or teased me by staying real far away. On those nights I would call to my mom, sometimes out loud, and then GG would appear instead and offer me a glass of cool tap water and another pill.

It didn't surprise me that my mother hadn't shown up since I'd been staying at Mark's. I imagined it might be all weird for her to visit at the house her former husband was now sharing with another woman. "Its okay, Mamma, I understand. I love you, anyway, even if you can't come," I said more than once into the sky where I figured she was sitting and watching all the commotion going on below.

On December 20th, I went to see Dr. Pigeon. This time my entire family sat outside, except for GG who refused to leave my side. The doctor kept us waiting for ten minutes, which gave me more than enough time to notice that my grandmother's hair had gone completely gray. I blinked to be sure it wasn't the lighting.

"GG, you need a touch-up."

Before she could reply, Dr. Pigeon entered the room. Dr. Pigeon without his hat.

He gave us a short greeting and sat on the little stool on wheels.

"Doctor?" I began.

"Yes?"

I motioned toward his head.

"Oh, oh yes, that's right." Dr. Pigeon reached behind him, into a drawer that he'd rolled open. He then put the cap over his hair, the brim facing forward.

I kept my eyes locked with his. "Are you saying its good?"

Although she looked utterly confused, GG kept her hands clasped like she was mid-prayer.

Dr. Pigeon broke a small smile. "I'm saying it's working, Chessie. It's working."

I leapt off the edge of the table and headed straight for him, giving him a hug he reluctantly accepted.

"We're not done yet," he said, into the back of my neck as he gently pulled away.

"Okay, okay."

GG was rocking an invisible child while her lips recited a silent salute to God.

I fell in love in that moment. I fell in love with hope, with time, with work, with the purple people eaters, and with a stupid Cardinals cap.

★

GG had managed to do some Christmas shopping on my behalf. She got Mark a boxed aftershave. I turned it over in my hand several times, wondering if it was okay. I mean, what was *the* right gift to give a father who dropped out of your life for so long you forgot what he looked like? I kept thinking about how GG used to buy the same thing for all the male teachers I'd ever had in elementary school when I'd pass from one grade to the next. Mr. Daniels, fourth grade, smelled like cheese. Cologne was hands down *the* perfect present for a man who reeked of rotten provolone. And Mr. Uliak, in seventh. We got him Musk for Men even though I heard he was gay and would have preferred something frillier.

"What do you think?" I held up the box and asked Logan, on the night before the night before Christmas.

"He'll like it, I guess," she said with a shrug. "I don't know… I got him a tie. He doesn't even wear ties that I can see. Gosh Chess, do you think this'll ever *not* be bizarre?"

"I'm pretty sure it'll always be bizarre."

"Oh good," she said. "I'm sort of getting used to things that way."

It was proof of how the human spirit forced to acclimate, will do so even if it means having Mark Madrid as your dad.

✯

"Your father wants to see you in the study," Anne told me.

It was five thirty on Christmas Eve. There was a spinach quiche in the oven that filled the air with an aroma defying the traditional fish frenzies my grandmother usually served up on December 24th.

I left her with a smile and she ran a warm hand across my back. We were far more than friends, far less than step-mother and child.

Mark's study was full of papers, books, and folders tossed on his desk, spilled out on the window ledge and piled on the floor. This was clearly not a room Anne had any say in. He sat in a black leather chair that resembled a big bear and invited me to sit, on a small overstuffed armchair beside the door. For a minute I was in high school, in the principal's office for being caught throwing my pudding pack during a lunchroom food fight gone wild. *What have you got to say for yourself Ms. Madrid?*

"I wanted to talk to you tonight, Chessie. Anne and I have been discussing the possibility of inviting you and GG to move in here with us permanently. If you continue to improve, perhaps you can even consider attending college in the spring or fall. There are some great schools around here." A small lamp at his elbow shot a shadow across his face. He hadn't been shaving regularly and his eyes looked darker than they once were.

"Mark, I-I don't know. I mean, there's a lot to consider. I'd totally have to talk to GG, unless this is another one of those things you and she were already planning secretly."

He shook his head. "Nope. This is something I wanted to bring to you first. There's no right or wrong answer. It's a matter of choice, your choice."

"I'll let you know."

"That'll be fine."

I stood up to go.

"Oh, and Chessie?"

"Yeah?"

"Merry Christmas."

"Merry Christmas, Mark."

✦

Logan and I were hanging out in my room, one week post holiday. She was reading a book from school that she said she had to do a 40-page paper on. I was reading a card I got from Meg with a photo inside of her and her new guy. It said, "Here's me and Jack under the mistletoe. Isn't he the hottest? He has a cute cousin for you. Hurry ho-ho-home!"

I'd been feeling a pull for the town where I grew up, for the streets, the shops and the sights and sounds I'd known so well. St. Louis felt a lot like the shiny, black leather boots I got for my fifteenth birthday, too tight and a little hard to walk in. Eden's Pond felt more like my tennis shoes, soft and stretchy with low, comfortable heels. I could run in them if I wanted to, run all the way home if the mood was right.

Mark and Anne wanted me to stay. GG said she'd do whatever it was that made me happy. Logan said it if wasn't for her dorming at Tulane, she'd probably want to live in this new place with this new family simply because she'd grown so attached to Max.

Everyone had an opinion. I needed something more and yet I couldn't be sure what it was.

"Chessie!" Anne was calling to me from downstairs. "You have a phone call."

I went into the hall and took the receiver in my hands.

"Hello, Chessie. It's Dr. Pigeon."

"Yes, hello doctor."

"I have just one word to say, Chessie."

"One word?"

"Remission."

I dropped the handset on the floor and then fell to my knees to retrieve it. "Did you say I'm in remission?"

"I did."

"Doctor Pigeon?"

"Yes?"

"I love you."

The inside of my head was buzzing with possibility. Just one word had put it there. My decisions were no longer a dilemma. There were none at all anywhere in sight.

★

It was time for Logan to go home to Louisiana to spend what was left of her school break with her aunt. She finally told me what it was that had the woman locked up to begin with, said she'd been caught with a whole slew of unpaid parking tickets. Though it didn't sound exactly right, it was the story she told and the one she needed me to believe. I did so because it was for Logan and she deserved nothing less. On that morning she put on the new plaid scarf GG and I got her, and we hugged one another as if we had been sisters forever. We vowed to call as much as possible and write when we couldn't. She thanked Anne for making her feel at home and Anne reminded her that she was at home whenever she was here. She kissed the baby on top of his head and turned to Mark.

"Thanks for everything, Dad." The room fell silent, and I could see both Anne and Mark fighting back their tears. She'd called him Dad. It was like we were at the restaurant having cinnamon waffles again. They wanted to beam and celebrate the way they had over Max's first Da Da. But neither one wanted to scare the moment away.

He threw his arms around her neck and gave her a polar bear hug. And just like that she was gone.

☆

Seven days struggled past. I spent them Logan-less and stinging from the loss. My afternoons were busy sitting on the floor playing with Max and his dozens of toys and my nights even busier looking for my rightful place to be. Mark came to me, one early evening, knocking at my door and asking if he could come in.

"Sure," I said, and he did. I was half sitting, half lying on my bed, and he grabbed a throw pillow, sat down and scrunched his long legs down to fit beside it.

"Anne wanted me to try and talk you into enrolling in one of those schools we talked about. I came up here to do that very thing. Yet...I can't. I can see who you are now, Chessie. If I gave you ten good reasons you might be willing to go along with it, though you'd be doing it for us, not for you. You want to please the people who come to you with their plans for your life. I'm amazed that a girl like you is related to a man like me." He looked up and outside. "You're exactly like she was, like your wonderful mother. I was such a fool, such a selfish fool." He was shaking his head. I imagined he was looking for her face, in the clouds, so he could tell her how sorry he was for his own bad choices.

"I don't think I can stay," I whispered.

"Will you be okay?"

"I think so. And no matter what, I will always know you guys are here, and this room is here and that I can come as much as I need to."

He nodded along. "That's right, absolutely right."

Anne would be disappointed. I hoped not crushed. She'd done all the right things. "Will you tell her for me? Tell her she's perfect."

"I'll handle that. Don't worry."

He untangled his feet and stood up. "I want to say, for whatever it's worth, …I love you, Chessie."

I looked down. It was harder to hear than I ever thought it would be. His hand was on the doorknob before I spoke.

"Thanks, Dad."

I heard him swallow loudly as he left me there, alone with my remission and the wheels in motion. I was suddenly smiling. I was suddenly flying planes in my mind. Mark Madrid had finally heard all of his children call him by his name of the heart. And I had my tennis shoes in my hand. I was going home.

## At Last

They'd opened up a new tanning salon in Edenville. On account of this Meg had an unseasonable dark brown tint in the middle of the cold, gray Missouri winter. She didn't care if people knew she wasn't off at some tropical island. She also didn't care if it was so frigid outside that your breath snapped and broke in two when it hit the air. She wore a tank top just to prove her point. Meg had always been more than comfortable telling convention where to go. But I think it was mostly to mask her insecurity, like a false, strange bravado.

"Do you remember me?" I showed up on her doorstep unannounced wanting to enjoy the look on her bronzed face. Her hair was pink on the ends.

She stepped back first and then forward, pulling me close and keeping me there against her chest that smelled like Vanilla Musk. "You really did it. I knew you weren't going to die. I knew you couldn't leave me."

Only Meg could make my impending death all about her.

"We have to celebrate," she said.

"Absolutely."

We caught up quickly, and before long, I ran into Johnny. He made some dumb joke and then some dumber comment about how I looked good enough to eat. The best part was that I felt nothing at all. No anger. No thrill. To my huge relief I had managed in the months that passed, to become Johnny-numb.

That very same day, Meg and I headed to the Dairy Maid. I

was going to face down Cole Harris for the good of all mankind. It was all the celebrating I needed. Meg egged me on. "Do it, Chess! Give that sick bastard hell!" We found him there, wearing one of George's old uniforms and a nametag that said, "Cal." He wasn't cooking or serving. He was the janitor, in charge of dirt. He didn't notice us slip inside, taking a seat at a table furthest from the counter. I waited until he was within striking distance and then I said his name.

"Well, shoot," he loped his spindly arm over the top end of a broom, "if it isn't Chessie Madrid. You lookin' all fancy now, like that black sister of yours."

I had a raging assault of words all ready for him, about the disease of racism and the disease of him. And then I remembered how I stood right there, one day long ago and assumed that all men had to have a cause. If so, then Cole Harris stood for lost causes everywhere. He was meant to be a lesson in how some people would never be kind, or sweet or ordinary and how regular people just had to learn to deal with that.

I simply smiled. "Welcome to the planet, Cal," I said, and walked away. Meg and I waited until the coast was clear and proceeded to build a mountain of ketchup, mustard, mayo, salt and pepper, in the center of each of the tables the new janitor was going to have to clean. Regular people and revenge made an awesome pairing.

★

The movie theatre was empty. I walked into the lobby of the Edenville Multiplex with an agenda that had nothing to do with the featured films. I told Meg I'd meet her at Shelley's at ten. She didn't ask where I'd be until then, and I didn't offer any information. Though this time it wasn't because I was ashamed. I didn't tell her because I didn't want to jinx anything. It was a little past nine and I moved through the room on the lookout for George. When I didn't find him behind the ticket counter or the snack stand I assumed he was off duty. I was about to go when I decided to ask. The girl looked a little like me, and she was shaking a gigantic bottle of salt into a vat of popcorn. I wondered if she was George's new senior, if she bossed him around and made him clean up the mess on the floor they way I'd done way back when.

"Hi, by any chance is George working tonight?"

"He's up there," she nodded toward the ceiling, "in the projection room."

I stared up at nothing. "Will he be there all night?"

"I don't know. But you can go see him. Right through that door and up the stairs."

I followed her directions and found the door to the projection room. It was closed; I knocked softly.

After a few minutes it opened. He stared at me, blinking once before he gave me a small, uncertain grin. "Chessie? What are you doing here?"

In the months since I'd seen him last he'd grown into his limbs. Most of his acne had cleared up and he'd somehow managed to tame the cowlick in front of his hair.

"I'm back. I'm back in town, and I came to see you," I announced expecting the fanfare would begin at any moment.

"Oh…" He said with far less adulation than I'd suspected. And then I heard her voice. She said his name in that singsong way girls do when they're obviously flirting and don't think they are.

"Geeeeeoooorrrggge!" She appeared next to him, wearing a similar get-up to his. She had long, shiny blonde hair and the biggest boobs I'd seen since Meg's. "I need help," she cooed in his ear.

"Okay," he told her dutifully.

"I'll let you get to work," I said and spun around to go. I was nearly to the bottom of the stairwell when he called to me.

"Chessie!"

I stopped.

"It's good to see you again."

I smiled at him. "Thanks, George." I guess I wasn't the only one who had made some changes. George was coming into his own, and that meant that he'd become attractive to females now.

It was proof of the way the universe felt about timing being everything.

"Maybe I'll see ya around," he said. It wasn't a back flip, but it was something.

"Maybe," I said and then left.

I went to meet up with Meg who was already hanging out with her new boyfriend who looked a little like a rock star with short spiky hair and a hoop earring in his lip. He kept calling her "babe" and she seemed to think it was the first time any guy had ever used that word. They were happy, and for a minute I was jealous that no boy was calling me babe. Then I thought that perhaps George was calling the blond girl babe. And then I wondered why I cared so much.

☆

In the weeks that tumbled past, I lived my life in a way I hadn't in a very long time. I stopped having to be pretend-well. I stopped wondering when the Big S would come calling. Most of all I forgot to worry about whether or not I had the right to any future plans. I signed up to go to that aviation school in the fall, the one I used to think I'd never be able to see. It was invigorating. I talked to strangers, cut my hair, and in a spontaneous act of freedom, spent one rainy early spring afternoon at the tattoo parlor outside of Edenville having a rendering of a pigeon drawn into my hip. I spoke to Logan nearly all the time. I spoke to Mark and Anne once a week. I thought about what I wanted to be when I grew up, now that it seemed I was doing just that. Pilot Chessie Madrid, the girl with wings.

GG and I reclaimed our home. We hired a professional to put a fresh coat of paint on all the walls and I enjoyed the strong fumes, even came to attach it to the scent of a new beginning. GG was happier than I'd ever known her to be, especially after a visit to Doc Abner's reconfirmed I was still in remission. She kept busy planning an Easter dinner party for the Madrids from St. Louis, Logan from Louisiana, and Mrs. Delafield from five blocks away. Anne was bringing the cranberry sauce, homemade, and a zucchini bread she said she thought I'd love.

I spring cleaned my bedroom. It was the first time I'd done so in years. I threw away tons of stuff, and found the retainer I lost when I was thirteen. At night I waited for my mother to come, to tell me how thrilled she was that I'd battled my disease and won. But all was quiet on the inter-wordly highway between us. Then one day when I was changing my sheets I came upon a card that had fallen in the space between my bed and the wall. It was from her. I don't ever remember her giving it to me. On the front cover was a picture of two hands, one big and one small. Inside she had written, "Reach for me and I am there. We are never apart, Chess." There was no date. I opened my vanity drawer, the place where I kept things I never wanted to misplace, and put the card inside, right on top of the wish list I made when I thought I was dying. I told myself that she'd found another way to communicate with me and it made the inside of my chest buzz—this time in a good way.

☆

Easter was quickly coming. I envisioned the little children of Eden's Pond searching for rainbow colored eggs hidden in the thick green bushes in their yards.

I could hardly wait to see Max dressed up in his sailor suit and testing out his sea legs. GG made a list of groceries and sent me off to the supermarket. The holiday was two days out, and she wanted to be prepared. I had just made it to my car when another one pulled up. It stopped right next to mine.

"Hello, Chessie."

"George…hi. How are you?"

"I'm okay. I was coming by to see you. I hope it's all right. I got your address from Patty at the Dairy Maid."

"Really?"

"Yeah. I hope it's okay I'm here."

"Sure." My hair was piled up on top of my head. I was wearing my gray sweatpants with the big ink stain on the knee. To top it off, I had slipped on my snow boots because I'd thrown out my left sneaker by mistake.

"It's good to see you again. You look real nice." He stayed behind the wheel. "Were you about to leave?"

"I was. I need to get some groceries for Easter dinner."

"Oh, well, I don't want to keep you." He shrugged.

"How's work? Are you still over at the multiplex?"

"Yeah, for now. I'm going to community college so it's only a part time thing, ya know?"

I nodded and stuck my hand into my pocket. My keys jangled, and George shifted in his seat. "So how's that girlfriend of yours?" I asked.

"What girlfriend?"

"The one in the projection room with you, the one with the big, um, eyes."

"Who—Lindsay? Oh, she isn't my girlfriend. She's only a co-worker."

"Oh." I nodded again and smiled.

"Well, I guess I should take off then if you have to shop." He didn't want to. I could tell straight out.

"Hey…you know you could come with me if you like." I kicked a rock out from under my foot and watched his face turn brighter.

"Yeah?"

"Yeah. Definitely yeah."

We took his car. And we went together, George and me. He carried the heavy bags and opened doors for me like a true gentleman. I told him how I was planning to learn to fly in September. He said he knew a guy who went to that school and that he could go there with me one day and show me around if I wanted to. I said I wanted him to. When we got home we put the food away and I made us instant hot chocolate and we talked. A lot. He thought his life was weird simply because his mother had two different color eyes and his father liked opera. He went to sleep-away camp every summer when he was a little boy and hated it.

He broke his nose from a fall off a horse and then broke it again from a fall off a ten-speed bike. His last name was Benson, like the singer—so cool. His favorite color was blue, favorite band was Genesis and he liked fried dumplings. And last but not least, he liked me. A lot.

Once I thought it might have been better if I'd been wishless, wanting nothing at all from this life except to keep it. I was wrong.

## But Not Least

I'm up to Day #7117. So far there's no end in sight. We're all going on with the business of living—GG with her pies either coming in or out of the oven, and her tissues still attached to her wrist. I check her eyes every now and then and they smile at me. Inside of her head she wonders when her own number will be called, when she'll move on and be with her husband and daughter. When she'll finally have to leave me. She never says so, though I can tell in the way she goes about tending her garden, leaving enough space for another tree to be planted in her honor first—not mine—the "order of things the way its intended" according to her.

Logan is becoming the writer of her own poetry. She's had three poems published in the university paper and one in a magazine that I've never heard of. With her words she reaches into the world of little children showing them the path to family and forgiveness and how it can have a very unique rhythm and rhyme. We're what we call "fristers" some recipe of friend and relation that is all our own. She isn't running so much anymore, although she says maybe one day she'll run for President. I figure she has as good a shot as any.

Meg is still charging through her life like paper on fire, changing her colors until she finds the one she likes best. She's on her fourth boyfriend since Jack.

Anne Darrow Madrid remains steady, overseeing her only

child, baby Max, as he grows into the man his father always wanted to be.

And speaking of Mark, he continues to chase the wind where he believes his happiness lies. Anne keeps trying to tell him, but he has to see it for himself—that it's right there inside of him, where it's been all along.

☆

George. George was the answer to a wish, an answer I never saw coming. We count our days together now—like there's a brand new calendar that's just for me and him. We're planning to fly to Hopeful, Alabama, with me behind the wheel.

As for the Big S—we've agreed to disagree. It wanted to claim me but it didn't know what I was made of way down deep, my mother's spirit. It didn't know who I was, who I am still; the roots beneath the tall oak, stretching, growing, pushing up and out through the concrete walkways paved over me. I cannot, will not be contained.

Doc Abner is semi-retired now. I'm practically the only patient he sees. Yesterday I asked him, "So Doc, what do you think? How much time do I have left?"

And he smiled and said, "I'm not God, Chessie. I'm guessing you'll have about as much as you'll need. Give or take."

He's got new hair now. It never topples over.

I want to believe him. But I'm from Missouri. I suppose that means we're just going to have to wait and see.

# About Author Louise Caiola

By day, Louise Caiola wears an Administrative Assistant hat at a local business in her hometown in Long Island, New York. In the hours that are her own she entertains the writing bug. Her short stories and essays have appeared in the online magazine FaithHopeandFiction.com. This is her debut novel. She is currently in the final stages of development on her next one. She invites you to visit her blog at http://louisecaiola.blogspot.com.

CPSIA information can be obtained at www.ICGtesting.com
Printed in the USA
BVOW010504281011

274545BV00006B/14/P